*TRANSI**T***

TRANSIT

by Rosaire Appel

FICTION
COLLECTIVE
TWO

BOULDER • NORMAL

Published by Fiction Collective Two with support given by the
English Department Publications Unit of Illinois State University, the English Department Publications Center of the University of Colorado at Boulder, the Illinois Arts Council, and the
National Endowment for the Arts

Address all inquiries to: Fiction Collective Two, c/o English
Department Publications Center, Campus Box 494, University of
Colorado at Boulder, Boulder, CO 80309-0494

transiT
Rosaire Appel

ISBN: Cloth, 0–932511–70–8, $18.95
ISBN: Paper, 0–932511–71–6, $8.95

Produced and printed in the United States of America
Distributed by The Talman Company

Illinois State University/Fiction Collective Two

On the Edge: New Women's Fiction

Also available in the series

Is It Sexual Harassment Yet?
by Cris Mazza

Close Your Eyes and Think of Dublin:
Portrait of a Girl
by Kathryn Thompson

A GLASS PUSHED AWAY IS ONE thing, a glass pushed over the edge is another. Someone turns to pick up the fragments, everyone else keeps on talking. One gesture bleeds into another. Some fragments draw blood it is only blood. How much blood has to be seen? Blood at the center of a hole, any hole. Hole at the center of a heart. At the center of a thought, at the center of a word—the pinhole through which life rushes.

Someone impatiently seizes the subject and sets it away from the edge of the table—so far from the edge that it misses the center, falls off the far side and shatters.

It is replaced by another.

Someone turns to sweep up the fragments—everyone else keeps on talking.

The cafe is crowded. Severed conversations circulate and converge, dissipate like smoke. At one of the tables, stubbornly separate, a young man toys with a glass—with a transparent restriction, a cooperative subject—his fingers slide down the wet cylinder mechanically. He follows the movement with his eyes. Repetition, simultaneous reflections, double voices—subjects and objects advance and switch places. Interception is part of the taste that is swallowed, the rest flows away unended, uncharted. Moving the glass around on the table, he blurs the rings as soon as he makes them—wet shadowy trance with no future. Or squinting through the glass-enclosed liquid that trembles as all confined liquid trembles, he measures the distance to the edge of the table, an edge both active and stable.

Against a background of tangled voices he remains transfixed by the object in hand. Or by the hand itself. His posture is casual, even lazy. You suspect he may not know what he is doing—lifts the glass, returns it to the table—a little closer to the edge. He nudges it with his forefinger gently, light flicks of local force. Then pressing the rim between his soft prongs he deliberately sets the glass into the zone where an accident is likely to occur.

"What's wrong with him?"

"Is he doing that on purpose?"

Ears tense against the expected shatter—the floor is tile the smash would be brilliant.

"...making a scene with himself in the center."

"To get your attention."

"Ignore it."

A dog meanders among the tables and the young man turns—the spell is broken. One subject recedes, another enters. A glass exchanged for a dog. A glass, a dog, a shrill voice cuts in: "Is it you! Is it really!" Two women recognize and embrace one another.

"They all look alike," someone mutters.

The lure of the peripheral, the bond of distractions— a table of contents could not sort it out. A table must have at least four equal legs, be tight and tried in the same definition day after day to be a table, no wobble, no matchbooks stuck under.

Matches, dogs, ice for your drink—conditions too slight for solo performance extend behind the scenes, unfulfilled, and bear down on subsequent occasions. One expects an outcome in spite of it. In every condition a future must follow systematically on the heels of its present, one insists. It must arrive with verbal promptness, be rationally consumed without anxious reflection—or vanish into its own wrapping.

But subjects and objects, conspicuous yet deceptive, are constantly exchanged, reforged or surrendered. Add handle and saucer a glass is transformed—it becomes a transparent cup. The sound as the cup finds the saucer's circle, the force of that cup being set down makes one start.

"Is she doing that on purpose?"

"Why doesn't she stop?"

"Why do you keep interrupting?"

"Ignore it."

Other people at other tables drink from more innocent vessels always and speak from more innocent faces.

HE PRESIDES AS IF ALONE IN THE room, as if there is no one here to notice. One thinks for a moment that his face is familiar, the torso under the crumpled shirt, the condition of his concealed aspirations, his guard—gray cardboard—cold sense of waste. A knowing evolved for protection—projection—description does nothing to alter him. If he is known through recommendation, one recommendation forsaking all others...but he skillfully evades detection. He evades. One can sense his complaint, his distaste for this moment by the flat, inflexible line of his mouth. But already he is starting to slip out of focus, neither memory nor fact can intrude.

A woman joins him, he does not look up. Her voice is warm and tame, a light fur. She positions this fur as if he is listening "...the men got down on all fours like dogs, yipping and whining, can you imagine!" Amusement makes her syllables tremble, one can't hear each word, just the texture of fur.

"I know who I am, I'm aware of the room, the people here, your face, I'm not ill," someone says in a low voice behind her.

Here is the line between cup and saucer, here is the limit of voices. Here is the place where volumes collide or retreat or defeat one another. The pressure of confinement, the skill of preventing—in any beginning: indulgence, some liquid—a cup and saucer or a glass.

O N THIS SIDE OF THE STATION
where he is standing the shade is excessive and stagnant and hot. You've seen him once, you've seen him daily, suitcase and brown parcel beside him. No other person in sight. All the benches have been dismantled, graffiti blooms on the wall. What is left of the tracks is buried in rubble yet the man stays vertical, in place, without pacing. You cannot say he is waiting, there is nothing to wait for. He comes back the next day, you do not see the point. He must have lost his sense of duration or some other crucial faculty of chronology. A balance within him has slipped. The horizon was false—fire plunged into water—you might say his curtains got singed. A trace of Western band music is audible, it is always late afternoon.

He is protected by the angle of the sun in your face, you squint, your eyes water, or there is smoke. A suspended net of motionless dust makes it increasingly difficult to see him. As you look he seems to dissolve. Or located in an increasing distance, the sector he occupies tends to expand. You seem to be using the wrong apparatus to try to make something out. Something about a man at a station, even I can barely see him. He has the substance of memory at this point—deceptive, transparent baggage.

The mention of memory induces a flux, intelligible if it is lifted slowly. *He was gazing at stones, at the rubble. The ground was white, not smooth but rough, the used surface of gestures erased.*

Subliminal refractions push to the surface to form a recognizable frame, enough to reconstruct a place, a face, a stance, appropriate scenery. Faces that are not one's own should be easy, more direct access and quicker to gauge. Stones that are sufficiently worshipped will gradually break out of their sturdy casing. Those stones, that baggage, both subjects and objects—gray traffic of content all around.

MORE GESTURES ARE PUT ON the table. More glasses and cups raised and drained. Drinking is a necessity for us, isolation occurs when drinking is cautious. The clatter of plates being stacked, spoons sorted, the constant drone of domestic activity upholds the surface and secures it. But familiar conditions decrease in value to eventually become invisible. In the background someone is reading aloud, another voice skimming another surface. "*Should you find yourself in this dangerous predicament you may experience relief and protection by placing a wet handkerchief or fresh plantain leaf in the crown of your hat, the ends hanging down...*"

Here the heat may be an advantage: one's hold is easily dismantled. Normal appetites become unstable, you find yourself drinking at any hour, you find yourself dreaming of strangers. You hear their voices wherever you go and cannot absorb what is happening. Yet happening is a distraction. It leaks into each moment—distorted, opaque. You cannot see beyond the distortion. A dog emerges from a shadowy corner, your attention undulates automatically toward it. Attention in this climate is elastic. Between the voices and the words you hear whatever you want.

I am sitting with her at one of the tables, postcards unfinished, swatting flies. "That fellow there," she whispers suddenly pointing to someone fondling a glass. Overlapping circles on marble that glistens, colorless forms with no center—"that man." Putting her voice very close to my ear she insists I hear some fact about him. Confessional urgency cradles her voice, I draw back but the cradle keeps rocking. Her smile no more than a scrim rebukes me: she will tell me whatever she wants. Dark trousers, white shirt, sleeves rolled to the elbow— I return to him for her sake—local shoes. As if he is listening she shields her voice from him, a whisper like cellophane protecting the story. She had gone to the place where he lives, she says, that room he rents from a friend. She knocked, no she looked in the window at him, blew on the screen—he didn't hear. He was moving around doing nothing in particular, on his feet, not sitting down. "He didn't see me didn't know I was there," she insists. "I couldn't call his name, he hates his name. He had said call me anything but Joseph. Joseph was all I had. He was muttering to himself or praying. The window was in the wrong place, I couldn't hear, he was facing the wall, no picture, no shrine. I couldn't see the point but I waited. I waited. Although there were chairs along the veranda, I didn't sit down, I didn't speak." She tips the teapot all the way down, black leaves flow into her cup. "But I might as well have opened the screen and looked him straight in the face."

"Shall I read the leaves?" I joke.

She sucks on the dregs saying nothing. Pushing her cup to the center of the table she gives no indication of returning to the present. She remains immobilized on that veranda where nothing will happen but what she admits.

Within reach are long strings of compatible words, read and recited by someone behind us. His particular enunciation suggests that the subject is not the object of his reading. *"In the cold stage of intermittent fever a marked fall of temperature may not occur..."* He turns a page that will not stay turned, picks up the book, cracks its spine. Flecks of glue spill out of the tunnel, he brushes them violently from his trousers. *"Strong light may well become intolerable in cases of acute affections. Infections acute infections. You would do well to resist the temptation to force your own way overlooking the patient..."* He is broad, middle-aged, consequential. I see him wherever I go. *"If the patient cannot endure strong light the room may be darkened to her satisfaction. But at times she may beg you to perform certain services which might be injurious to her. She may ask you to open the window for instance when the window ought to stay shut. Through some slight ruse, rearranging the romans—the venetians, rearranging the venetians or curtains. She can generally be led to suppose that you have actually complied with her wishes."*

Having abandoned our conversation she settles back no longer resisting the advance of nonverbal attractions. Her chest expands slightly, contracts, pauses, small waves of air passing though unattended. A familiar transaction with just enough force to generate a semblance of participation in the time rolling out all around us.

Released attention circulates outward. In the street other throats are swallowing oysters—in the cellar mice gnaw at the laundry. No one appears to be full. Some bodies leave, others enter. One reaches toward, one listens—or doesn't. Either way the time passes, any time, on its own. Light from the background intensifies or diminishes. But here in the mind there is no coy rheostat easing the site from light into dark. A first glance is obliterated by a second and so on. Subsequent visions are variations, replicas contaminated by memory and desire.

The shape of a day is easy to hold: light is elastic, darkness is firm. Then darkness advances and becomes elastic—daylight turns brittle and shatters.

THE STENCH OF BURNED RUBBER
coming in through the window blends with dull sweet
shades of tobacco. The haze is pulled in and pushed out
by all in soft habitual spurts. No one is creating a
disturbance. No one is insisting on being an example for
everyone else to follow.

He taps the pack to extract a cigarette, positions his
lips around the filter, strikes the match, draws up his face
in a squint meant to shield his ocular membranes from
wayward smoke that would sting. The persistent craving
of any habit provides a gestural frame for the future. A
craving persuades one to enter the future by preparing a
place for oneself in advance. How easily one can come in
and sit down at a table, any table, because of a craving.

"I'm the one who suggested the trees," a voice resumes with authority. The person is obscured, just his
voice exposed. "*My* trees are replacing the trees they
remember so thoroughly that they forget what they
knew."

"They all look alike."

"You are blind."

"When I arrived I made an effort to suspend preconceptions, to withhold all judgement..."

"Of course you did we all did. We had to. We surrendered our initial intentions, we..."

"This place combined with corrected descriptions of places toured in the past is the present. The present takes place in the present, you know, nothing can happen without hindsight."

"Your tone of voice is unbearable!"

Move your chair or turn your head—the scene is replaced without being disrupted.

"We went to see the view from the hill in this heat and then that rain!"

"Are you ill?"

"I've always liked a distant horizon, vast parallel planes that can't meet. I've always liked the fact that the sun touches nothing as it slinks through the curtains, touches nothing as it stains the floor, how it drops so patiently behind the sea—uncontaminated, uninfected by all..." Audible punctuation—fear of conclusion—she breaks off with a chronic laugh.

"I find your naked horizons chilling," her companion eventually retorts. "Infinite desert of sky and water, that line that illusion of meeting, no thank you. There's no reasonable explanation for anything at that point—an absence of perceptible history, no thank you."

"You don't..."

"But I do all too well!"

The chemist is pushing his way through the crowd, they too know him by sight. He is slight. Eyes, tie, belt, wristband, everything about him is narrow. They wave to him in return for a nod which may or may not have been meant for them. He joins the uniformed men.

Buckets of sand hang from spikes on the wall. A lantern swings menacing pendulum shadows beneath each spike within range, then is still. Beyond this soft-tissue artificial light another night develops full strength. Feelings that cannot be canceled entirely force uncertain objects to surface again. The subject forks or stays on the plate. Pick up a glass and finish the drink.

"Postcards sent to other people confirm the existence of other people. Native costumes and winding streets..."

"But your script is impossible to read."

"The obligatory message: some fat and some weather, write love, add a stamp and your life is extended. An act of will, aggression, not affection, an act of willing infection." She grabs a newspaper from the next table just as a man sits down.

"You may have the paper, I have my book," he says with the clarity of a memorized phrase. His meticulous voice gives each word equal weight, I recognize this as well as his face—two sides that begin to close. I...

Dark photographs weight the front page of the paper, professional captions deliver the sting. The texture is uneven, grainy, shade both excessive and stagnant. You've seen him before, the parcel beside him...

Her companion abruptly calls out to the waiter, "Hey Joseph, what's for dessert?"

Joseph approaches their table. His eyes are a little too bright, too quick. A limp shirt sticks to his ribs.

"Nothing but water on this menu," he tries. Words tossed out of an empty bank. Then roughly grabbing a chair by its shoulders he swings it around and sits down. "Nothing but biscuits and water, ha ha!" Too loud, too long, he is noticed by others. Not for the first time he pulls us toward him, coaxing us to do something about him—resist him, blame him, kiss him, arrest him...

"He was gazing at stones, at the rubble," he says. "The ground was white, not smooth but rough."

"Your tone of voice is unbearable!"

"Subliminal refractions push to the surface to form a recognizable frame, enough to reconstruct a place, a face, a dance, a ladder of fact..." He laughs without visible amusement. Nothing can touch him as long as he uses words lifted straight from the page. He continues in the same lofty voice. "Faces that are not one's own should be easy..."

Dropping some coins in the saucer, the two women rise. They leave *Joseph* holding the paper. I look down at the table, avoiding his eyes, several long seconds of suspension follow. The sharp sound of coins on the saucer echo as the setting resumes its familiar torpor. The audience returns to its previous connections—his presence begins to dissolve. Even before he throws down the paper the incident has ended.

But I notice he is not returning to the kitchen, not stopping at other tables, he is leaving. No doubt he is not a waiter but merely...

A meticulous voice, a dry, closed circuit, moves like a shadow into the foreground. A shadow is merely some shade in transit, a plane of parallel, unconnected, absent light. His voice is merely sound in transit moving steadily over old tracks. *"Secretive, undertone conversation must be strictly avoided in the sickroom. Nothing is more calculated to alert the—to alarm the patient—than whispering or murmuring behind his back, making sig-*

nals *he is not meant to see. Do not let memory pervade your—mystery, do not let mystery pervade. You should sit where the patient shall see and comprehend exactly what you are doing at all times..."*

A sinking sensation steadily repeated is one of the ways one preserves what one knows. *Hey Joseph, what's for dessert?* Sensations that cannot be altered by will, desires unratified and blending with others. He'll remain disturbed by that echo, no doubt, while the rest of us languish in comfortable silence, settled in comfortable chairs. The subject changes to chairs. The object is often relief. Significance meanders like oil on water, unstable marks on a shifting surface. Comfort is apparently the condition demanded, or relief, when one craves a different sensation.

Tracks to uncharted directions continue, conflicting fascinations, a voice tightly wound. Anyone passing might admire that voice artificially sustained in a window—in passing. The intrigue in some cases is the force of the winding, indulgence inhibits recovery and so on.

Indulgence placed within view and removed, recovery again and craving. It is difficult not to give up and walk out when no single craving takes over the rest.

SOME CRAVING PROWLS BENEATH the surface—pending, opening, slipping under the others. Arranging the history of its own voice, rearranging its furniture, engaging in thirst...

"...she said she was standing in front of the window when someone called out get away from the window. She jumped back, she didn't know who shouted. Her son was in back in the yard with a shovel. The trees had ejected trillions of blossoms into the pit, onto the rubble—she may have said ditch, even grave. He was doing his fair share and more she complained—he was her son, her only begotten, the father had long since departed. She said he had left without breakfast that morning, said he seemed nervous—the son, not the father. Later hearing his voice in the street, she ran to the window—she laughed when she said it. 'Mother throw down my valoun' she mimicked. In her mouth the *mother* was crude, sacrilegious, a shape like a battered kettle. She yelled back she couldn't find it, he'd have to come up. 'Look under the bed.' She refused. She wanted him to come up and have supper, sleep in his own tidy bed. Poor woman has never managed to learn there's more than one to way hold a needle. When someone screamed 'Get away from that window'—no that was quite a bit later. She went back to the stove, she was mad. The next minute she thought she had won. She knew her son couldn't bear being wet, even the wet of bathing annoys him. She was sure he was on his way up. She was sure..."

"Everyone says the same thing."

"But he couldn't go up those stairs, he told me, something in him refused. At times like that he hates his life with a primal violence that nearly destroys him. He crossed the access to the cafe. What did he care in that state! All he could do was drink. He drank. He drank and watched the door. Drank with one hand while the fingers of the other drew splinters from the edge of the bar. After a while he sat at a table. A second shot did nothing to still him. He was certain his mother was coming. To taunt him, shame him, drag him back in—the nerve of her voice would be taut with his name, straining to pull him back through it. He was sure she knew he was here. He allowed himself one more shot. His heart was racing as if he'd been running, he paid for his drinks and stepped into the street, changed his mind and ducked into the cellar. There's a ladder in back, an exit to the alley, he could take the back streets across town. He had a friend or two he said, he knew some independent people. But he heard his name being called—heard her voice by preference or compulsion. Her voice with its harrowing demand on his person—his name enclosed in that voice now stunned him, he was unable to move. As if he were merely her private opinion, a duplicate copy of someone living—then he lashed out cursing the worth of her life as though he himself wasn't from it. He said he knew her bed was sturdy, he said he had seen where she hid her locked box—and what cheap things she kept in it. His eyes slid to the top of the stairs. All around him were unopened crates and cloth bags of sand or flour. Mice were frisking in the laundry—he was struck by how nervous they were. 'How stupid they look,' he said. 'I myself will no longer be nervous,' he announced aloud in the cellar. As if no one had met him yet, as if he knew how to will. He made that vow and intended to keep it, that moment alone in the cellar."

DRY LEAVES, SMOKED PAPER, A
trickle of voices seething through laughter, cold oysters,
heat—above his head in the cellar.

"Good men in trousers are not the same as men in
good trousers," someone says, others laugh.

The chemist comes in by himself but he leaves. Four
others come in, no one knows them. Their trousers have
cuffs, their shirts are flat, they are not wearing local
shoes. One of them asks the price of a drink—the other
three keep their backs to the wall. One pinches sand from
a fire bucket and lets it sift to the floor. He does it again
and again without pausing, a compulsion affecting in-
creased concentration. Having abandoned communal
allegiance he freely conducts this separate performance
while the others stand ready, arms crooked at the elbow—heat radiates from them like gas. He is curing some
internal discrepancy no doubt, the others are watching
the door. A dog moves in and out of the shadows—the
waiter threatens to kick it. Outside at one of the shaded
tables a woman is writing a letter. A hand-written sentence so easily opened—but can she bring it to a close? It

cannot be abandoned, it is there. She studies it. Seeking conclusion, seeking circulation, the sentence that must be finished so that...

A disturbance across the road in the grass becomes more pronounced, they all turn to see it. A flash-line ripples through the green, more evident in movement than actual body, flame in this light is transparent. What is consumed is not the new grass but a line slicking toward some dry sticks, wadded papers, propped up at the base of the statue. Children jump up and run toward it laughing, the men in good trousers rush forth with sand. The children grab fistfuls of stones from the road that they hurl at the statue, the men heave their sand. As if the limestone is going to explode—but nothing explodes, light passage of smoke.

It is over as quickly as it started. The men in good trousers are laughing and drinking including the one compulsively sifting. Someone says are they heroes. Someone calls them assassins. The barman says nothing at all. An elderly man makes his way through the crowd and addresses them formally, asks who they are.

They laugh in his face. "Don't you recognize us?"

The old man peers into their faces.

"Are you friends of my daughter?"

"You don't know?" one man sneers.

The old man seems confused, turns back. "Let him pass," someone says. They continue to taunt him.

She gives up trying to finish the sentence, only to take it up again. She does not know who these people are, who the statue resembles—why blow it up? It is merely a statue of a uniformed man with some weapon, she doesn't know what, in his hand.

"They all look alike," someone says.

She has no sense of local history nor how prettily it dovetails with other histories. A statue of indifferent stone.

"*T*HE DOOR OF THE SICK ROOM *must be kept closed, a sheet soaked in chloride of lime hung outside...*" As if reacquainting himself with the language, he reads aloud, not tending the center. "*The head is thrown backward, the throat projects, the face becomes flushed and the eyelids tremble, but the jaw remains firmly closed. There is no distortion unless the patient is uttering dreams of—screams of exclamation. Though time conceals a wealth of symptoms...*"

His internal voice interrupts. *To speak in a manner that indicates wealth, a basic black sentence is all that is needed.*

"*Boxes and trunks must not rest on the floor. Place a layer of stone or stumps beneath them. Even your beer-bottles cut in half...*"

Bringing his hand to the level of his face, he examines the palm at close range. *Indications of fate or arbitrary intersections, either way my hand is my hand,* he thinks.

"*...will prevent small reptiles and irritating insects...*" Sweat trickles into his eyes, he stops reading.

When she comes back with a pitcher of ice, he acts as

if it is a different morning. A surge of kindness, evidence of hope—each time she comes in with the tray. Then the kindness and hope are contaminated by dread, false trust, the rest unravels.

"Don't bother, I'll do it," she commands. She moves efficiently, without special attention. He fusses with objects on the bedside table. "I said you didn't have to bother," she snaps.

"Thank you." Now he is humble. "Weren't you telling me, no I was reading, no, that's not what I meant to say, never mind."

She vigorously mixes some powder with water, the clatter annoys him, he sucks on his teeth, ties knots in the fringe of the spread. As she meticulously adjusts the venetians, effortless constructions of words stream from her. "Eventually he went back to his mother, not that evening but several days later. For the first time he noticed she was old, she had shrunk, was thin as cardboard and shoddy. He himself was tall and bold—*she barely had strength to put plates on the table. Stop twisting that fringe it'll break.* What had kept him from noticing her gradual decline, no doubt, was his extravagant resentment of her. Her voice long confined to the heat of one room had dried up and turned fitful and brittle. Her words broke apart, he couldn't piece them together. When he asked her to speak more distinctly for his sake she smiled bravely at the hearth. In this way she forced him to come nearer. Coyly decreasing the radius of her voice she drew him to the hearth where she stood, at the mercy of primal intentions. He had no choice but to go: she was weak. He stood beside her facing the mantel, her hand on his shoulder, his shoulder enduring.

She was carping about that hole he was making, sick trees, that statue without its head. Attaching her voice to words of false safety, she lured him toward the original landscape. He didn't see where she was leading him this time. He slipped back, his eyes turning dull and listless, his mouth shut like a trap."

"Is there anything—is there more ice?" he inserts the moment she pauses.

"More ice?" she echoes.

"More ice?" he mimics. "Must you repeat what I say?" he charges. As if his voice contaminates words, hers cleanses them like disinfectant. "Just bring me the ice," he shouts.

An empty moment follows his outburst, they both know there is no ice to be had. She fills his glass with water from the pitcher, his breathing gradually turns even. He finds himself facing this same separation, sentence after sentence in the silence that follows, the same door closed in his face.

His hand moves backward, under the pillow, he pulls out the keys he keeps there. His own keys.

"Keys continually carried in a pocket retain their brightness, don't need to be polished," she says from the other side of the room. He hears her disinfectant voice, squeezes the keys in the palm of his hand.

His legs are stretched in front of him, arms hang slack at his sides. Locks that have been forced are useless, his locks have been repeatedly forced. His mouth is pinched, his eyes dry. Resting her hand on his arm with light pressure, she continues the story of the mother and son. She stretches their images across the ceiling, across the window and door. No escape. Her voice soaks up all sound, all air. His breathing turns shallow again.

The moment she leaves, he coasts backward. Indifference settles like dust around him, one thought dragged down by another and buried—the futility of trying to prevent it. He disappears from the surface completely. Not until his body rebels is he forced to open and return to the world. He finds it is daylight again, or still. He is not sure how long he was gone.

Trying to recall, to sort it out, out of duty, he fingers small objects on the table—the curious articles she keeps by her side, whose function he cannot explain. He opens the book he was reading. *Gloves must be wrapped individually in tissue, placed in a wide-mouthed jar and corked well. Needles must be protected from rust as must pins in any damp climate.* He turns several pages at once. *If the lamp should fall to the floor there exists a strong possibility of danger. Burning oil will travel quickly across the rugs and up the curtains, up the stairs and into bedrooms where your young children are sleeping. For this reason sand must be kept in buckets or in covered boxes that may double as ottomans. All candles must fit without the addition of paper wound at the base.* His eyes are drawn to a stain in the margin, he forces them to return to the print. *Passing a light in back of the head producing a shadow—for less than a second. The hand holding the lamp must be ready, small articles kept in a box by the door, a light moth spread over the body. Light cloth. The body which is about to be buried...*

He snaps the book closed. It falls from his hands.

"A simple intestinal weakness, it's nothing," he murmurs in the empty room. He finds himself facing the same separation, breath after breath in the silence that follows. The door behind him is closed. The curtains are slack at the window. Time passes through him from pocket to pocket, time that fits firmly and time that wobbles—hot wax spills on the red floor.

AN OFFICIAL'S ROOM IS DULL, low ceilinged, with uniform windows outlined by plain molding. Within is a table saluted by chairs, his files, his certificates—nothing to degrade him. Nothing moves but black specks that are flies. Stick trees and rubble beyond the windows are bleached by a light that knocks out all shadow. Light so thick it smothers the day, each day in its quest to unwind.

He is struggling not to unwind. He paces. When his restlessness deigns to abate for a moment he stands still waiting for it to continue. The familiar churning resumes, he paces, as if he is trapped in this room. Considering the strength of his occupation and the significance of his medical condition, I say nothing to him as he paces. He has sat in each chair, I presume. I finger small objects spread out on the table—his presence deteriorates to mere decoration. His objective character relieved of its duty empties itself, he is still.

I wait.

He comes to with a start, repossesses the room—stocked folders, stacked ash trays—expectation, confirmation. Focus requires frequent adjustment, flexible chords let parts pass in and out. He makes an effort to erect his old part, to re-establish the appropriate convention. But disturbing allusions to personal matters flow horizontally beneath his intentions, threatening to break into the open. Threatening... Then sound flows into his being again—a bird on the sill, footsteps in the hall. Sweat collects on his neck, in his hair, he wipes his hands on his shirt.

"I will go to the clinic tomorrow," he mutters, words unnaturally thick in his mouth. He attempts to dilute them with water. The strident voices of his desires have always conflicted with both memory and duty. He pours again, gulps it down.

"Thirst is sometimes just thirst not a symptom," I say, feigning innocence—he starts. He had apparently forgotten my presence.

A current shoots through him, forcing him up, he looms across the table.

"I appreciate personal favors," he states, authority leveling his voice. "A personal favor is not the same as an act of mercy—what am I saying?" He tries to cover his confusion. He picks up a postcard, "This, explain this." He waves it at me, I fold my arms. He places it on the edge of the table—as if it's a bone, I'm a dog, it will tempt me. I have had enough of that postcard. As he continues to ply his authority I tickle the card with my shoe till it falls.

"What are you doing?" he cuts in. I glance at him without sentiment look away. He bangs his fist on the table. I fix my eyes on his with a stare that makes him start pacing again.

"One day is the same as the next," I venture, "one

season all seasons together. One day you remember to wind your watch, one day you forget and die."

"Imagine whatever you like," he retorts. He stops pacing, looks at me sternly. Obediently fixing my eyes on his, I continue saying what he wants to hear. "A wedding car passed, I remembered it later. I remember graffiti inside the station, blue paint on dry ocher, blue paint on the trees. When I got to the highway, I flagged down a bus, the wedding car passed it was dusk."

"Go on."

"They came down the path, large men dressed alike, skin bolted firmly to their bones. Helmets instead of skulls. Trained to camouflage personal humor, traveling in packs, speaking in unison—one of them spotted an object in the thicket, yanked it out and threw it to the ground. The most striking feature was the care with which the thing had been constructed. For rabbits, I guessed. They laughed. For dogs? They encouraged me to examine it closely—do I have to explain my reaction to it? Why did they think I knew what it was? I had gone to see the view from the hill, the scene on the postcard, your imaginary horizon. Later, wanting something to drink..."

He encourages me to include more detail, what was I wearing, what was I thinking. He assures me he has plenty of time and he wants to hear it—he wants to sink in. He wants a conclusion that is revealing and laced with disturbing implications. He longs to be disturbed.

But perched on the edge of his desk—his large body— he is the one who continues talking. He cannot entirely disregard the fact that I make him aware of his private content, his emotional contours, rough breathing, his volume—raw substances mixed with desire.

I turn and look out the window. Because of the smoke it feels like dusk, all afternoons are like this. The sky injected with the fat of our lives turns sullen and bloated, a stench comes with it.

Although increasingly uncomfortable with me, he seems unable to stop. He forces himself to keep to the task of uncovering a particular significance he craves—one never craves what one has. He suspects I have figured in a few of the dreams rising up from his infected heart. Dreams now motionless, fixed in advance: imprisoned fantasies, ready-made and repeated. He believes his past is successfully finished, the surface clear, no scratches no stains, not even his fingerprints on it.

"I have paid for what I have," he announces, "paid for what I bounce without quitting. Others count blossoms that fall. Do you prefer to bounce a ball or do you prefer to count blossoms?" His laugh holding neither surprise nor delight is conventional fluff, soft pellets expanding. He struggles to avert peripheral distractions beginning to encroach on the scene in his mind. He avoids the rest of the paragraph he started, one sentence with roses and applause, one with silk. His eyes tear from the smoke. The room is noticeably hotter. The fans have stopped, his soaked shirt draws flies, he slaps his calf, his temple, his chest, his motions becoming frantic.

Finally abandoning the situation he steps onto the balcony, I watch in a mirror. The light like live coals hits his face, he shrinks back, cowers in the dank shallow shade of the wall. The stench is making him gag. As if there is mercury expanding within him, his temperature rises, his body trembles. He is dreading the course it will take this time, dread squirms in the pit of his being.

Dread works its way toward his solar plexus, shoots through his veins, he sinks to the tiles.

I am not here to catalogue his symptoms, it is *his* mirror not mine. His mouth contorts to accommodate a yawn that refuses to come into being. His mouth opens and closes without sound, like a fish. A transition, a losing of form.

But even artificial acts are revealing. I call out to him softly, "Are you ill?" Doesn't answer. I pick up the postcard, return it to the file, fold the file into my purse and go out.

Afternoon slides into evening, smoke slides into bread without butter. The binding condition is torpor. Evening requires a relocation to some other site for something to drink, waiting for clocks to unwind.

Drinking ideally in a place of one's choosing, not required to be somewhere else. Not required to be there for someone else. Not required to be someone else in that place—in a room with black specks that are flies.

IN THE PAPER IS A PICTURE OF children in the road pitching fistfuls of stones at the statue. Before that there were flies on their lips. Before that they were singing songs for the mothers, today they saunter like soldiers. Children are so pliable. Moving eagerly from table to table, four or five have banded together. They stop at her table to sell her a paper, she shakes her head no, she bought one that morning. She points to the paper tucked under her purse—a fat straw fishlike shape with handle. Suddenly the tallest boy seizes the purse, runs off, the others scatter.

It is over so quickly it may not have happened. She turns to people nearest her—no one meets her eye. She jumps up and rushes outside. She is seen and she is deliberately not seen, conversations close in behind her. One season all seasons together and so on, one day the same as the next.

Released attention circulates inward. "She was mistaken, nothing happened."

"No doubt the heat is why she was swearing."

"What are you going to do next?"

"When does the train leave tomorrow?"

"Not tomorrow, it's a holiday, I saw in the paper."

"It's always like this, I hate to travel."

"You're tired, it's indigestion, it's nothing. The milk was sour—you've had this before."

The conclusion is an extension of the same afternoon. Her newspaper stays where it was on the table, a still point in the midst of circulations—words diverge, dissipate like smoke. The original disturbance produced a wound, but wounds heal, the sky eventually clouds over.

She crosses the access at an angle. Here is a man drawing lines on the ground, lines that have no shadow. Another is digging with a shovel. Yet another is carting stones away. In her ears is the buzzing of flies. The stagnant heat, and the light that comes with it, curves a mood under, dulling its contours. Like dust suspended in the air, there is movement without explicit direction. On the other side men are passing the bottle, day after day in the same direction. By evening they move like aquatic plants pushed forth by invisible currents.

This section of the access is marked with string that is tied with ribbons of rag. The ground is intentionally smoothed over. Approaching it from the side of the village, one suspects that something has been buried. But approaching from the official residence, one has the impression that grass has been planted. Positions change, implications reverse. Some people say the windows have *grilles*, others call those same verticals *bars*. The officials are healthy and benevolent—the officials are equally angry and pale. They wink at each other in gilded mirrors—they wink at the facts, they wink at the polls.

Forefathers are kept in the halls. Bouquets erupt from high-shouldered vases on all the tables in all the rooms. Decorative jars filled with ash mark the steps that lead to the upper, balconied rooms.

Now a man appears on a balcony, leaning heavily on the rail. A dull light clings to his skin like waxed paper— she continues crossing the access at an angle and does not notice anyone at all.

ASUBSTANCE LIKE CELLOPHANE shrinks around him, sealing him in a tight sheath. His chest has no space to expand. He believes he is standing in front of a mirror—a stench of burning, ash-rites, accusations...

Then forcing an encouraging yet artificial smile—public, reproducible, neither personal nor endearing—he regains enough strength to waken slightly. He moves his hand to the side of his face. "I love you," he whispers into the mirror, more drama than sincerity, more echo than claim: memorized reassurance.

He wipes his mouth after saying it.

Finding his legs in working order, he opens the door, goes out. It is night. Quadrants of light from neighboring windows leak onto the ground, corrupting the dark. It is darkness beyond all light he craves now, a limitless sweep in which nothing exists. He turns his back to the light. Facing the darkest and most distant location, his jaw finally relaxes, he is able to yawn. The possibility of authority returns. The light behind him is still offensive, but now it seems unofficial. He himself could dominate that light just by thrusting his body into it. His foot in the eye of that light—but he stops. A sound alerts him, he is not alone. On the veranda a few feet away a chair is ticking like a clock. He thinks for a moment that snow is falling, slow soggy flakes, he shivers. He stares at the area of impending activity, unable to see anything distinctly.

"Who's there?" he calls out in a voice so thin it turns back on itself. Someone else is speaking. She seems to be giving a list of names, living or dead, they mean nothing to him. He does not keep track of who lives who dies, he barely keeps track of himself. Yet, as if she belongs on his veranda, she rattles off names like accusations. He mentally crosses them out. The outrage from possible recognition, the heat from stirred embers...

Or successfully blocking his imagination, he hears in the distance an engine being started. It stalls each time it is started.

"I expected you'd come out," she says. She recites his name, his clinic number, political preference and so on. He gives no indication of hearing. Between them a balance locks into place, each side holding full to its own.

He wishes he had stayed in his room. No one had forced him to come out—why can't he go back to before he came out and not come out this time? As if expecting to be transported back to his room, he holds his breath, becoming increasingly enraged. *Time needn't be so intractable*, he fumes. *Everything else can yield now and then, it's stupid to have such strict rules, it's unfair.* He has the impression of clouds rising up, the softness of lips, hair cool as snow. An ancient commotion surges within him, breaks through to his heart, flows into his bowl. The malice that floods him is stern, yet warm. Here finally is something he can touch. Stepping into the light, he advances quickly, joining her on the veranda. Before she can speak he seizes her arm, pins it behind her—she screams. He holds the moment a fraction longer, but her voice is broad and intelligible. A shutter opens upstairs. He lets go of her arm, she springs from the chair, leaps over the rail and is gone.

The place she occupied is immediately empty, the chair perfectly still. The silence is so overpowering that he feels he has turned to stone. Then the stench of burning rubber comes through and a truck in the background backfires. A dank earth-smell seeps up through the boards, recapping his imagination. He has returned to his room. Staring at gloves in a jar on a shelf, he sees fish for just this occasion. He fumbles with the lid, it won't give. He picks up a fork and changes his mind. He abruptly yanks the sheet off the bed and hangs it over the window.

AN ENDLESS SHUFFLING OF familiar sentiments continues at the cafe. Some people leave, others enter. Beneath the limpid drone of voices is the clatter of knives and forks being sorted, the rattle of glasses brought up from the cellar, domestic proverbs, trapped flies, no ice.

"He went into the room where his daughter was sleeping, she sat up immediately and asked what was wrong. He grumbled that nothing was 'wrong.' Then bring me something to eat, she ordered. Can you imagine? To her own father! I'm not your waiter he informed her. Then what are you? *I'm* the one who should be in that bed while you, it's your turn to straighten the pillows. Sturdy hatred in both directions. They glared at each other without speaking. Menacing as wire attached to explosives—no thank you, I said, I don't have to hear it. I made sure they heard me go out."

"Elaborate reworking of unpaid accounts—can't she force him to stay at the clinic?"

"Everyone says the same thing. Dishonest work and attacks of fever should not be equally regarded."

"Yet to witness that routine denial of affection, to suffer because she..."

"You mean because *he*."

"Some people need painted statues of themselves as well as certificates of achievement on the wall. The sheer quantity of praise they require displaces everyone else."

"But he was the one, it wasn't her fault."

"Inner lives swell up under pressure, erupt with revenge, explode in their faces. The emerging substance is sticky, cloying, not something you want to swallow."

"He was the one who was sick."

"Some force like god sucked the air from his mouth and again he nearly collapsed on the street..."

"Allowances made for everyone here, made under the weight of a boot. Why not have pity, I ask you? If sexual liberties are freely granted, no subjects condemned, no advances rejected..."

"If enchantment becomes more important than comfort..."

"Take the person he had been as a child, for instance, respected by others, bathed in cold water..."

"Ignore him."

Others stare into space without speaking. The unifying substance is malleable. The degree of tension is continually shifting, it registers automatically on unstable reflections that tremble as all confined substance trembles. The surface reflects wayward light. The surface is thin impenetrable skin—condensation conceals the rest.

"**I**S HE GOING TO PUSH THAT over?" A voice as brittle as the glass that would break.

"Ignore him."

The hand continues to slide on the glass, up and down, a movement sustained by moisture, implications that may or may not be intended—does he know what he's doing?

"Ignore him."

"Restlessness only partially enclosed gives public access to private conditions. Gestures not weighted by social function depend on the presence of others to judge them. Should context be ignored? Should sex?"

"Take the person he had been as a boy..."

"Ignore him."

"Someone exact and impersonal for others—for himself, no more than a length of string pulled on and twisted by everyone else. Approaching the age of sex and money, he experienced the usual destabilization which eventually empowered him. He believes he is able to walk out of a room, any room, any time, if he wants by this time. You can tell by the tilt of his head his tight jaw: he is about to get up and walk out."

His hand addresses the top of the table in a rhythmic code of quick taps. A woman approaches, he stops. His hands—what of his hands in her presence? His fist inadvertently grazes his thigh, he hastens to brush off his own touch. His agitation increases. He positions his hands in full view on the table next to the slippery glass.

She has joined him without being invited.

His face by this time reveals a new surface, more difficult to read, more independent. He has neither embraced the new situation, nor given up the old and walked out. Conversations close in all around.

"Considerable taste and skillful arrangement are part of every successful denial, as well as every attempt to feel better..."

"Elaborate reworking of unpaid accounts, accounts for what gets done in the dark..."

Seeming to shift his private agenda into a less conspicuous mode, he forces an outline of himself to appear, a new rotation begins. Any outline is influenced by expectation, counterfeit hope—any outline so thin. One gesture could peel it away, one soft word—which no one is ready to say.

Independent of her and everyone else, his hands move to various parts of his body, his pockets, his hair; he massages his neck. The hands like screens, self-screens that patrol him—selves with their own private entrances to him. Protected momentarily from climatic intrusions and protected from himself by this clutter of gestures, making himself ready for her. He nods. A movement without his entire consent, perfunctory, lacking conviction. He flexes his lips horizontally. A horizon between false charm and humility is all that presents him to the world.

She begins talking immediately. Talking to cure certain sinking sensations, curing oneself while neglecting the other—but her voice is too light to follow. She speaks to him and watches his face—her intensity blocking his concentration. He looks at the wall, at the window.

Retreating into someone not quite himself, a makeshift guard, stiff boots bind his feet—he asks her to ask him again. To repeat. If he could see himself would he quit—his useless gestures, his useless retreat. But she asks him again, he advances a smile, and in this way agreement between them begins. Bones and skin keep their bodies upright, words keep them pliable and separate.

"The outline of a bird on an opaque window—that's all I remember," he offers. The memory spontaneously ignites another, which he accepts, he gives himself over. He believes that memories are harmless distractions, incidents clouded by distance, nothing more. As he speaks of the bird and the opaque glass, he sees himself at a window. The bird flies off, it is dusk. Once this has leaked through, the location opens, he slips into it without caution.

Water drumming on metal, that drone, the beaded curtain between the rooms, himself on the rickety couch with a drink, his feet on its arm, straw mats, a fat urn. Feeling substantial and in control he unlaced his boots, kicked them off. *I will be the authority here. I will determine what happens between us.* The lack of resistance, the excess of clearance—he strolled through the curtain to where she was bathing. The floor was wet from the make-shift shower set up against the back wall. He laughed. Your carpentry is pathetic, he told her, washing himself at the sink. He went into the bedroom, lay on the mat, a towel wrapped at his waist. She was standing by the window smoking. Someone yelled up: Get away from that window! She moved away quickly without explanation.

When she sat beside him, he pulled himself up and drew her into his arms. "Is this what you wanted?" he asked. He blew on her earring, she said, "Don't." The earring was a small painted parrot perched in a flimsy hoop. He blew again, it swung. "Don't." When he did it a third time, she pushed him over, took off the earring, 'Is that all you wanted?'

He leaned back on a pillow, playing with the fringe. She played with the earring in her hand. At that moment he saw a bird at the window, at least in his memory it appears at that moment. *Put on your pants and walk out,* he was thinking, crossing the room to the window. The air was dank, an immovable robe separating him from everything else. He could not touch anything through it.

It was his turn to stand at the window. "Let's go somewhere else," he said fetching his pants. She obediently put on her dress. He was willing to accompany her out of that failure—the failure to fulfill the unspoken expectation that was born the moment they met.

Leaving together they were two separate people, solidly isolated from the world and each other. The failure, having detached itself from them, kept pace between them, an autonomous articulation. It accompanied them all the way to the access, lost itself in the crowd.

Here were the festivities they meant to escape, the throngs of people knocking against them. His body was shoved against hers with a force he himself had not managed to achieve. She laughed and he did not condemn it. Illegal vendors sold oysters and liquor, the women were waving biscuits on sticks, others waved strips of rag, bits of rope. Moving wildly among the people were children, screaming, whistling, singing. Here local residents and tourists alike were exposed to similar sensations. Cold oysters slid down their warm throats and they laughed—shrill spiraling warbles moving outward. Contorted faces appeared, disappeared. He draped his arm on her shoulder.

"Do you live alone?" she asked.

He tried to squeeze by, "As far as I know."

"I've seen you with a woman often."

"It's finished," he said very quickly. "A woman who wanted me just for herself, without history, she wanted me empty."

"And you insisted on keeping your history."

"Of course I did, I'm not desperate you know."

"Tell me what's in that history of yours."

"I've often dreamed of exchanging my luggage for someone else's—shall I try yours?"

"Exchanging your luggage?"

"Must you repeat what I say?" He removed his arm from her shoulder. The crowd continued to push them together and now he pushed back, elbows extended, urgently hardened against them. The acrid stench of burning rubber was making him ill, but he could not stop breathing. An habitual version of external reality seeped into his innocent blood. Then, flowing back through his hidden history, a sediment settled at the bottom of his pit. That pit, alternately full and empty, was what he kept falling into. A trap continually reset and waiting, bait changed without warning, location made random. But by moving quickly in the opposite direction, he believed this time he could bypass the danger. He steered her away from the crowd.

Yet once away, he walked alone, as if she were not at his side. His attention, at one point, was drawn to a window—a sheet tied across it, the ends past the sill. Somewhere in the distance a truck was started, rough exhalation and choking—then silence.

Farther on a figure lurched out of the shadows, he could not see who it was.

"Is there someplace to get something to drink around here?" The voice asking was listless, resigned.

"Give me a light," the man persisted.

It was she who responded by striking a match and thrusting it at the intruder. He sucked up the flame with arrogant leisure, while the flame moving quickly along the match devoured the stem she was holding. She dropped it still lit to the ground. She said later she was sure he had done it on purpose—his eyes had been fixed on hers the whole time. He was trying to get into my soul she had said—his eyes stark, gouged into a hairless skull. She maintained there were men passed out all around, discarded, soft bricks that were useless. 'You and I,' she had said, 'are here together.' Then she put on his jacket went up the stairs, clad his life as if she owned it.

"The outline of a bird—is that all?" she breaks in. Her voice pulls him through the remaining sequence so quickly that it is as good as erased. He finds himself at a table with her, twirling an empty glass. Vertical lines, stray implications, glisten on the surface, are reflected at the bottom.

"The more slowly a substance flows down the throat, the greater the pleasure derived from it."

He moves toward her ear as if to reply, blows on her earring instead.

"Don't," she says right away.

When he does it again, she takes off the earrings, sets them at the center of the table. She continues telling him about the old men who were down on all fours and barking like dogs. An incident disabled by his inattention—she breaks off abruptly: "What are you doing?" She seizes the earrings that he has taken and twisted into each other.

"You did it on purpose," she accuses.

An investigation escalates between them, more accusation than anything else. Lack of precedent makes them incautious. Their eagerness to compete with each other and have the last word, cancels all others.

Yet the act of arguing provides opportunities that augment their initial goals. Each has possessions, both active and inert, that are challenged by the presence of others. Possessions that have their own lips, their own subjects, their own tracks and traps to be set or unwound. Additional objects still wrapped in warm flesh are hidden innocently within them.

He abandons his glass, his arms on the table.

"I know who I am, I'm aware of the room, the people here, your face, I'm not ill," someone says in a very low voice.

A FLEXIBLE CONTRACT FOR understanding extended through decades of privileged despair—wound and unwound like a string on the finger, colorless string picked up from the floor. She drops the string, folds her hands on the table, fingers twined, palms pressed together. The other woman continues reading aloud from a thick tattered book.

"If you have proper regard for your dogs, you will visit the kennel at least once a day to make sure they are adequately fed. But do not keep a fixed hour for these visits or your keepers will be on the lookout for you. They will make arrangements for your visit and prevent you from seeing the true state of affairs..."

She relights her cigarette from the candle between them. The reading voice shows no sign of stopping. The sound is compact, impenetrable.

"Bicarbonate of soda added to milk will delay its turning for quite some time..."

Desire for engagement being no less intense than the craving for cigarettes or for personal enhancement—another form of oblivion for some, a fine mesh trap for the rest. She gathers wax that has fallen from the candle, kneads it into a ball.

"Feathers will not keep their curl in this climate. Pins and needles will rust. Elastic will last but a very short time—make arrangements with suppliers you trust."

Pressing the wax, keeping it soft, she molds a miniature loaf. Appendages appear, nail dents for fur: the wax becomes a translucent dog. She destroys it the moment it is finished. Reshaping it into a featureless cube, she sets it decisively on the saucer. Her companion looks up from the book.

"Aren't you listening," she accuses.

"I'm out of cigarettes."

"Out of patience is more like it." Disappointment, resignation. She scans the rest of the chapter. *"It is not uncommon to discover a nurse whose medical knowledge is limited to local remedies and superstition but..."*

"Is stubbornness the opposite of patience?" Crushing the empty cigarette pack, she sets her words against the other's. "I have to go out for cigarettes."

"Going out at this hour, you're foolish."

She looks around for a clock. The candle illuminates nothing but the table, the walls have retreated into the dark. "How can you bear such large rooms?"

"I thought you would find these passages interesting, I thought you would like..."

"What I'd like is to borrow a pair of trousers, dressed like this—how late is it?"

"You'd do better to go without cigarettes this evening and stay with us for the night. But you always do what you want." Resignation, disappointment again.

She leads the way with the candle. The hall is wide, not closed at the ends, the darkness has room to expand. It swells without stirring the air. Although they are alone in the house, they lower their voices and stop speaking completely as they approach the back rooms. One goes in with the candle, one waits outside. No light remains behind.

Muted stirrings are audible now as the darkness weakens, shapes form out of nothing. A rocking chair, a trunk resting on stumps, underfoot are cracked tiles and pebbles. The prevailing stench of burning rubber blends openly with the damp plaster and dust. She stands without touching the wall. The rasp of a drawer slid home ignites a series of what-if proposals. *What if he comes back while I'm here. What if she mentions—if he should ask...*

"Why don't you come with me?" she hears herself saying, back in the room, stepping into the trousers.

"Going out for cigarettes in the middle of the night is not my idea of amusement."

"Must it all be amusement?"

"If you think that just by changing your clothes..."

"You're angry."

"No I think you're foolish."

She returns to the table alone. The racket of dogs barking in the distance delineates space, situates the near. Sounds that are nearest are self-inflicted, she refills her cup from the mottled blue pot, takes the sugar cube from the far saucer. Long shadows follow her hands.

Rearranging the candle for reading, she returns to the refuge of familiar structures advanced by familiar words. *During the intervals between the attacks, the diet should be wholesome and plain.* Reading as effortless as swallowing water, secure intentions, agreeable confinement. *Meat is the article most susceptible to indifference, while fresh fruits and vegetables that are prettily prepared...*

Suddenly the flame is sucked violently upward, as if by some unseen presence inhaling. It sputters and quivers, nearly splitting in two. "It means nothing," she says with prim authority to some other self within. But the quivering continues, a marionette flame—then stops as abruptly as it started.

She returns to the book, to the word at her finger, and treads the lines horizontally again. Lines soon blocked by internal extensions, pushing outward, splitting her concentration.

You shouldn't have lent—whatever possessed you?

An occasional glass of pure filtered water does wonders for many annoying symptoms.

It isn't uncommon for a woman to dress like a man if she must go out at night...

Must is the vortex of the sentence. Was hers a true must or was it desire pressed into a convenient mold? She wanders farther from the page. Dogs still howl in the distance. More words flow under the bridge untended. The soft side of her intelligence meanders: *A dog who barks has a home to protect, a dog that doesn't bark has none.* The subject splits, the current reverses, she abruptly returns to the page. *A small quantity taken in the early morning if sparingly admitted is usually harmless.*

Going out in the middle of the night for cigarettes is not my idea—is usually harmless.

Due to a lack of regular exercise the body, especially

the digestive organs, may succumb to a dangerous state of torpor...

Anyone out at this hour is fair game, both men and women plying the shadows.

The flames travel quickly up the curtains, up the stairs and into the bedrooms where your young children... She secures the candle in its socket.

Children are so pliable.

The hour is carried by erratic divisions, first one side is favored and then another. If she favored just one direction, she would find herself back at the entrance perhaps—or at an arbitrary exit.

SHE ORDERS A GLASS OF THE carbonated urine that passes here for beer. She is idle, more idle than anyone around her. Her slight physique and flexible posture are conspicuous alongside the hard-shouldered men. One man detaches himself from the rest, speaks openly to the side of her face. "I saw you this morning at the market." She appears not to hear, he touches her arm. She jerks away, he repeats his words—more privately, his confidence undiminished.

"What of it?"

"You were opening a—you were standing in the shade and opening a—unwrapping it slowly, I could see the seal, the impression on plastic, the..."

"And so?"

"What made you conspicuous was the slowness of—while everyone else was frantic. You actually looked calm. Oblivious. You seemed..."

"You're confusing me with somebody else."

"I don't make that kind of—I don't make mistakes." His voice is smooth, confidential. "I know your father quite well."

"Who do you think I am?" she demands. "My father has been dead a long time."

"Your father is at the clinic, I've seen him. You often entertain him with little stories, more skill than truth, to enrage him."

"Those who have leisure time can imagine whatever they choose to imagine."

"He has told me some of your stories. He has even confessed that he can't tell the difference between what has occurred and what you make up. Whispering into his ear like a ghost, those nights when he..."

"My father is dead."

"You decided that he was dead, so he died—still functioning, still believing that you would return..."

"A sun that sits in the sky is one thing, but a sun that comes out of your own short pocket..." The rest of the sentence evaporates. She asserts her profile, she has finished with him. Yet immediately she offers him a cigarette.

"No," he says, "she'd know I'd been smoking. Even if I rinse my mouth, she smells it on—it gets into your hair, your clothing, skin, it's amazing how smoke—nothing penetrates more deeply." Continuing in the same conversational mode, he is the one defining the route, determining how much scenery shows and how wide the middle will be. He controls the diameter of the gaps between words, between subjects and objects, he speaks without rushing. He acts as if he has earned the equation that came into being the moment he saw her, an equation that has been solved. "She attributes my smoking to selfishness, nerves—a pendulum shadows a course of distraction. She claims that whatever I touch I destroy, but *I'm* the one who planted those trees, *my* trees are replacing the trees they remember."

"All trees look alike."

"My child you are blind."

"The usual offense. The usual discount."

"Your father would say the same thing. I know about trees, I know about fathers. One day a father mislays his glasses, the next day his portmanteau is missing."

"You didn't know him."

"A truth only superficially grasped remains a truth nonetheless."

She turns from him, no longer listening.

He continues. "This morning for instance as I was shaving, still half-asleep, on the verge of dreaming, the shaving brush leapt out of my hand, as if someone had actually reached down and grabbed it and hurled it to the floor. I was—you can imagine. A brush is a definite object—and mine, I use it daily. When I—naturally, when I picked it up I examined it closely, the bristles were sideways. I straightened them up, but something had changed, it didn't feel like the same brush. I put it to my lips, I kissed it..."

"Don't tell me your little intimacies!"

"Then don't tell me your father is dead," he snaps back.

"He is dead."

"An elderly man can be made insignificant. Give him a corner to call his own a little away from the rest of your life, far enough so that he can't touch it. Give him a cup or give him a cap, depending on the strength of his skin. No matter how thirsty that father may be, the cup he is given is small—and it's yours. The liquid that quenches his thirst is yours. The cap that covers his head is yours. The father turned into a son who is yours—the son who originally named you—yours."

"No."

"An elderly father no longer goes out, he busies himself with pins and needles, he works in the dark, he is frugal. He keeps an old jacket over his shoulders and hides his keys under his pillow. He transfers them to his pocket. Keys continually carried in a pocket retain their brightness don't need to be polished..."

She turns to leave, but his hand darts out, encircles her forearm and holds it. The flesh is pliable, small bones near the surface. He tightens his hold—she laughs in his face. "Certain restrictions are imposed by knowledge, others by innocence, others by complaint. You can blame the weather, for instanc,e not the future, blame the fruit forgetting the soil. The difference between the tough and the tender is the difference between chickens and dogs." The rhythm of her voice, using words as if foreign—he loses his place, cannot follow. She continues to talk very fast. "Inaudible chords repeatedly struck, secret sounds prolonged in a living body..." She looks at him steadily with the force of a challenge.

He looks past her to a bucket on the wall.

The cafe is crowded, layered conversations circulate and converge, dissipate like smoke. Bodies press in on all sides. Casually letting go of her arm, he takes a cigarette from her pack on the bar. Positions his lips around the filter...

He believes he has plenty of time to decide which course he will chose this time. But the tone is already shifting. They remain without speaking and the tension between them weakens in the absence of words. She is already open to other voices, already treading some other current.

"They're not impressed by convenience, you know, they're impressed by extravagance, which is vulgar back home. They dream of coming to places like this—to describe them when they get home."

"Is that where you were in the downpour—don't tell me!"

"Dreams are impressions sinking like tea leaves, later uncovered and meticulously decoded—specialists peer into the cup, that same cup..."

"In the beginning, they don't want to drink, it but when they get home they want nothing else."

Putting his mouth to her ear, he whispers—she whirls around. "Do you think you're god?" she demands. "Do you go up the stairs in the dark, do you dare?

"What stairs?" he retorts. "There aren't any stairs. I'm not familiar with the tactics you're using but one thing I can say for a fact is that you..."

She turns, he reaches out to hold—she slips into the crowd and is gone. He turns back to the bar alone. Behind his head is a picture or citation or a line of improbable trees. To the left is a bucket of sand on a spike in a wall once white that has yellowed.

Nothing resists, nothing tries to fit in, a ploy as persistent as any plot. Ground is readily nothing but ground, breeze from a little heat over it. Crucial information, initially tidy, is altered the moment that anyone enters. One speaks of heat, one speaks of fate—the bartender washes his hands. A young man picks up a glass and drinks, sets it down near the edge of the table.

"History begins the moment a process is emptied of meaning from one side not the other."

"Is he going to push that glass over?"

"Ignore it."

"Hindsight is not the same thing."

Resigning one's place to some other body, one goes out the way one came in.

BEHIND THE NEWLY PLANTED access some men are passing a bottle. It is mid-day or shortly thereafter. A woman is walking a thin line of shade at the edge, pace slackened by the weight of the heat. Chaotic fluctuations of masculine banter, hoarse coughing, and a plaintive doglike whimper—her heat-dulled senses are alerted. It does not actually sound like a dog. It is coming from an old man down on all fours, the others holding their bellies are laughing. He sniffs the air for a scent and whimpers, continues crawling toward her. Long gloves, white hat—she is unmistakable. She refuses to hide who she is. She continues walking as the dog comes closer, panting and whimpering, his head at her knees. Without the slightest flicker of acknowledgment, she holds her course, makes him invisible. He refuses to be made invisible. Mock arguments break out among the others, two men sprawl on the ground as if wounded, moaning and sighing at her feet. The dog bends over them, licking their faces—the woman sees nothing, as if it is a dream. None of it registers on the surface.

"Let her pass," one says, they start howling.

Just as it seems she has escaped he lurches forward, his flask in her face. The open shirt, exposed throat-hollow, the broad pulsating cords of his neck—nothing, she sees nothing at all. She passes around him as if he is caged, his flask uselessly raised in mid-air, his laughter turning uncertain. She goes on. A corner turned, the scene disappears—she will never see them again. It is finished.

But even before she turns the corner, she has already circled back to the scene, passing among them as if she were dreaming, gradually making them visible. The circling is effortless, it happens without her, in fact she is powerless to stop it. His open shirt, the exposed throat-hollow, the pulsating cords of the neck of that dog, whose face is already becoming familiar, the face of the face of...of course she wouldn't know him.

Eventually arriving at her destination—her usual pot of tea and newspaper—she studies the paper with interest. She sees the open shirt, the throat, flesh as intimate as the flesh of a husband. The picture spontaneously reappears on every page of the paper. Yet she does not raise her eyes from that throat to see the mouth and eyes that go with it. It is only later, well into the night, that eyes and mouths will propose themselves, an endless series of possible faces to bleed in and fill out, not all unfamiliar.

The searing heat lacks warmth and compassion, even the shade is unsympathetic. Although she is sweating, she shivers. The same afternoon keeps moving around her, an expanse without markers on a shifting foundation.

It abruptly turns into night.

Awakened by dogs barking in the distance, sharp yelps followed by incessant yapping, she relights the bedside lamp. The intimacy of the wavering light confirms the distance between here, this room, and out there, the world where dogs roam. *A dog that barks has a home to protect, a dog that doesn't has none.* She sips directly from a small bottle, leans back on the pillows, eyes closing. For the first time she gives in to a fantasy that has been gathering strength without her consent. She pictures herself at home. The place called home starts out as a sentiment small as a slide, but eagerly focused. It illuminates the whole room. She sees herself unpacking the trunk and washing her hands in the porcelain sink. The soap does not reek of disinfectant, the air does not stink of burning rubber. She has her fruit trees and baskets again, the sheets her grandmother hemmed. An abundance of detail fits into the picture, she enters it fully, is safe in its lap.

From that place, she describes her present location to someone pleased to listen. The strange customs, sick trees and gray rubble, the statue, the market, the postcard view from the hill. Several characters come to the fore—but she is the one who has placed them this time. The power to erase is seductive. One incident that continues to vibrate—but even this is eventually subdued—a translated landscape emerges. Saturated with light, though not limited to day, the new version is neither exotic nor morbid. It is the place she will show. Setting this version in place of the other, she finally drifts back to sleep.

In the morning she returns to the practical rhythm she established when she arrived. A day advanced through strict routine is difficult to measure, easy to leave. When she lets the days go more easily now, she is picturing herself being home. If she stands at a window looking down at the ground, the ground is sometimes nothing but ground. Yet time—unengaging, an impersonal intermission—no longer advances, but expands.

THE AIR IS DAMP AND THE CARD-
board match bends as it is torn from the book. The stub
is too short to strike. Throwing the matches vehemently
from him, he grinds them in with his foot. "Give me a
match that will light!" he shouts. "Give me some peace
of mind!"

"Matches are cheap. Peace is fragile. And you have
the wrong kind of mind for peace."

He wads a page of newspaper. Hurls it at the fence.

"*Your* peace is the kind that sneaks up from behind,
fondles your nerves to make you relax, then gushes in,
overtakes you," she says. "It drives you into a frenzy,
your peace, you're too fickle for anything peaceful."

Encouraged by nothing more than caffeine, he tells
her how they had barked like dogs down on all fours, they
had nipped at her heels, and the woman had walked right
through them. His voice is taut with annoyance.

"She would have confided in me," she insists. "If
something like that had happened. You're making it up—
I don't have to listen. I offered you supper—fish, bread
and butter—but I don't have to listen to your stories."

"Generosity is irrelevant. You suppose it has virtue, good looks on the books—I despise your looks and your virtue."

"What don't you despise in that frame of mind?"

"The truest impact of anyone's influence is the moment when one becomes curious," he replies. "All your sentiments have the same axis, no leeway, no progress, no possibility. You don't make me curious in the least."

"Indifference disguising fear. A common technique for transferring strong feelings from one part of the psyche to another to avoid..."

He is shredding a cigarette as she speaks, hears nothing but the ease and authority of her voice. He prefers to drift without being secured and she does not let him drift. *Subjects twisted by vanity or complaint, distorted to fit like bricks in a wall—one version with blame, another with guilt, enough to finish me off*, he is thinking. *Each little cell with a curious expression, each little twinge of dormant passion...*

Bits of paper float down from his hands, white blossoms cover his shoes.

"*When the patient himself can't pinpoint the symptoms, but complains of a general loss of power, or as they say, want of tone,*" she says quoting, "*he disguises his fantasies as revelations and sets them out, solid properties, facts. One cannot deny...*"

"I'll deny what I want. It's you who pry, who take pride in tearing it all to bits."

"What makes you so critical?"

"Is that what you find so likeable about me?"

"Is that what you want, to be disturbing?" She stares at him with some definite motive, encouraging him to surrender. The dialogue, having stopped at her question, intensifies as it stands still. The internal pulse of the question quickens, explodes between them, and vanishes.

"After we're married I'll tell you," he jokes, is met by a look of indifference. "I've never lived anywhere but here. I've never been anyone else," he reminds her. She shrugs as if he is lying. "I'm not impervious to the luxuries of peace, ice for my drinks, shoes that don't leak. I can walk by your side without walking out—I know what you want me to say."

"I'm leaving at the end of the month."

"Why not settle here?" His tone turns sarcastic. "Why not spend your life making pretty lace shades for the lamps in our bedroom?" he laughs. "I am after all an experienced male..."

"Experience is nothing compared to the efforts that enduring affection compels one to make. Take love for example, take hate for that matter..."

"Love and hate are arbitrary conventions, mere props that keep everyone going."

"In fact, I could come to dislike you."

He rips another page from the paper, balls it, tosses it over the fence. His balls another and tosses it to her, she lets it fall at her feet. He tries it again, his expression turns hard. He draws himself up like a column. "I too have dreams!" he announces.

She looks at him. "Why are you screaming?"

"Do you know what dreams are?" he shouts.

"Dreams store and purify personal history. Dreams— you don't even know what you want."

He tears off his cap throws it down. Pulls off his shoes

and flings them aside. "Do you know what dreams are?" he shouts.

"I have a fixed job, a good cook, and free weekends," she says, retrieving his cap. "I make sure I have plenty of light when I read, and when I am hungry I..."

"I'm not attracted to light, it disgusts me. I'm not attracted to reading. To read is to walk in another person's shoes—they cramp your toes, they pinch, you limp."

"Reading is a generous act, but you're obviously loath to surrender yourself. You prefer your own moods, your precious dislikes. Pushing them past their sociable limits, you brazenly snap them in everyone's face. In this way you attempt..."

"Your cook buys dog instead of rabbit and you don't even notice the difference. One rabbit in the center, square dogs all around—I know you're thinking I'm crazy." He is holding his breath. She breathes calmly.

"We have no real history together," she says quietly.

"History is an imaginary line..."

"The moment that one becomes curious—that's history. A confident version of public events developed with hindsight and logic—that's history. A line inserted into the past, pulled out and read like a thermometer."

"I require nothing, I like sleeping alone, in fact, I think I prefer it," he replies.

"Common history is what we are here for."

"To pass time between dust and dust," he counters.

"Time is not just a perceptual device, it is also the agent that tricks the mind into wars over chickens and eggs."

He throws the rest of the paper. She continues pushing sentences at him, extending them past their normal limits, building some parallel situation. As she speaks he tries to pull himself up through layers of inertia and mistrust. But the layers are opaque, he cannot pass through them. Her words flicker and glow. Certain sounds are diverted, random sentences collect, some spoken, some whispered, as if in a dream. He hears an incantation of voice devoid of both content and motive. Sometimes at night alone in his room her voice returns like this to haunt him. Sentences scatter across the ceiling—are swept clean by the headlights of cars.

She finally stops, he does not know why, knows only that she is no longer speaking: her verbal invasion has halted. He hears an unnatural silence. Alone with himself, that same self she resists—he looks at her directly. She rubs her arm where it had been twisted. He kisses the flesh that she rubs. Then he lays himself out on the bench like a corpse, she sits down on the ground beside him.

"I've never liked being surrounded by water," he confesses, as if the true subject were water. "The weight of it pressing against me, the pressure, the slippery texture..."

She says nothing.

"Water is too universal," he continues. "Impersonal, not like milk. Take a tub full of milk instead of water, straight from the udder, a cow in the shower..." He laughs by himself, still alone. Sweet odors from dreams blend with his laughter, he touches her hair, strokes it like fur. The present becomes too thin to grasp and escapes without his noticing. He envisions himself buying oysters. He sees a man on the station platform. One image delivers another in a sequence that is unpredictable. In this state any image is effortlessly inflated—then the air escapes, the flesh sags and collapses. He never experiences a natural conclusion, just the collapse.

She is sitting on the ground, he is prone on the bench. Raising himself on one arm, he smiles—his teeth, like bars, imprison him. He sits. As if a dark cloth is suspended between them, her expression is entirely concealed from him. He stands. She does not move. He rattles the fence impatiently. He needs some motion other than mental, this constant revving of secondary motors, the innocuous doodling resuming upstairs... "I'm leaving," he announces. She says nothing.

He walks away without looking back.

She continues sitting on the ground.

H E CAN SEE WELL ENOUGH without switching the light, carelessly enters his room—but stops. Someone—dark profile against the window—he conceives she is not an illusion. He leaves the door open behind him. Intruding on him is a memory of her: she used to arrive like this after supper and read aloud from her foreign books, and she had seemed pleased to do so. In place of his own private whisperings then, she had given him actual sound. She had brought him companions, albeit elusive, but he could forgive them, convinced he was different. Characters told and retold in one voice—doors that always closed in his face. He generally liked dialogue best.

Now he slams the door against that past, as if she is an illusion. He feels his face, his definition—her back to the window, her face is in shadow. Another situation begins to unfold without a foreseeable destination. Disagreeable options are detected and removed before they have time to develop.

Or it seems to him there are no options, the outcome has been solved—it is fate. He is a prop, a bystander without influence, not actually living, but mechanically existing because of her presence.

"Aren't you glad to see me?" She finally speaks, her voice still soft, but dry. She holds the words apart from each other, separated sounds, forbidden to touch. That moment in the vague light from the window, an unusual glow on the sides of their faces resembles the heat from the tension between them beginning to rise again. Although she claims to have loved him too much, he remembers her loving him quite a bit less. She had called the less lapses and let them exist, while he held to a love both strict and inflexible—intensity she no longer deserves.

He throws off his cap and turns on a light with a single gesture, suggesting a motive. He embarks on a passionate objection to the heat, the lack of dependable plumbing and so on. His protests are comfortable, habitual, ineffective. He clears the cups and saucers from the table, puts out a plate of cold biscuits.

"You look well, you seem recovered," she offers.

Without knowing why she has come at this hour on this particular day, he replie,: "Is that what you've been trying to say?"

"Is that what I've been trying?" she repeats. He recognizes her with these words. She has always given back what he says, returned his words in her self-possessed echo, her voice transforming both passion and fact, turning the porous opaque. Making the true artificial. He will never accept his own words from her mouth—-dead words litter the ground. Live flames leap up from dead words in a second—how easily she ignites them and fans them!

He slumps into a chair. "What hasn't already been said?" he asks wearily. Warning himself not to force fate by rushing—yet anyone attracting rumors as she does, at a time when danger is carried as casually as keys are carried in a pocket, he is thinking. Grit in the air gets into his eyes, which he wipes impatiently, unless he is crying. "Is it true native women aren't affected by heat? This cursed, this noxious, unnatural climate. If I'd known beforehand—you realize this, don't you, this kind of heat is not impersonal. It mocks every gesture, destroys every..."

"Excuses common as flies—the heat. Solitude for over a month, I have heard—solitude that was not advised. I recall you saying that you would not try..."

"I never recall," he interrupts. "I'm only interested in what hasn't happened." He walks around to her chair. Insects lash at the screen. His memory and some mysterious longing like seasons, all seasons together, have force. Thus far his longings have been discreet and limited to encounters he could survive. He has never consciously wanted to die, never consciously craved destruction of his self by the self of any other—a version he insists on still. He has done many things for her sake, however, which were not part of any longing. And when she described certain patients to him, he had listened for her sake, not his. The image that remains in his mind of those patients is alarming, he refuses to consider them. Locked doors, locked windows, locked hands. Good patients are given short pieces of string that they wind and unwind, their useless fingers. No other distraction is offered.

Now he searches the cupboard as if he is hungry. "I

remember one patient who used to amuse you..."

"I didn't come to be amused..."

"I don't care why you came," he says loudly. "Why should I care why you're here? You've already left, you're a ghost, a mirage—blink and you're gone, vanished." He snaps his fingers and laughs. "This isn't happening, you've already left, it's a scene without figures, just props." He jumps up and opens the door. "I'm just coming home for supper." He reenters the room as if alone, sits down and takes off his shoes. He picks up a newspaper, reads aloud: "A spoonful of dirt is worth money. Excavations provide more jobs. A minor explosion marked the anniversary..." He throws the paper to the floor. He is making himself more alone in her presence by speaking into the air. "Initially she was my only distraction, but she has switched places with everything else. Now I only want everything else. Go on, I don't care, why wait?"

He lies down on the bed in the corner, his hands rest on his chest. Insects lash at the screen. Yet even as he holds this course, he begins to drift back, this version dissolves, another slips into its place.

She has not yet arrived, he is waiting. The night is opaque and condensed as he left it, two figures are barely visible. One of them is still walking away, the other still sitting on the ground.

A LAYER OF TIME IS SPREAD over each day, a duration enforced by hourglass sand drawn downward through a pinched neck where it settles, inert—until someone turns it back over. Daily he consents to turn it over, starting at the top, it seeps to the bottom. A rhythm of rain, a rhythm of reading. Yet when he craves a different sensation—and a less familiar extension of himself—his dislike of this time, this mock location, erupts and spills into the void that surrounds him. Familiar gestures drain his ambition—symbolic figures, reversible captions—why bother to be here at all? He consoles himself with thoughts of departure, set up without effort, not easily cancelled. The moment he finishes what he started, he will leave—or the moment he leaves will finish it. Each time he turns the hourglass over, each time he threads his way back to the present, reinterpreting the captions, figures, props... Renditions as seamless as sand piling up, sand moving over the same ground daily, advance followed by retreat. Yet he is determined to witness a conclusion and will furnish what he must furnish to have it. The persistent low-grade disappointment he suffers generates enough irritation to sustain him.

Thus, despite the heat and his residual boredom he feels obliged to see the view—the naked horizon that tourists praise from the hill, the postcard attraction. He sets out well before noon. En route he mentally adjusts his itinerary: learn more about their medical customs, vegetation, the birthplace of the mayor—and what of that rumor about the chemist, his wife, that business at the clinic?

Idle inquiries, idle sand, idle heat.

Though the hill is not steep, he climbs heavily. The soil here is baked and bleached, trees emerge to die. Annoyance, avoidance—held in suspension. By the time he reaches the parapet, the view, his throat is parched, he is straining to breathe. The air is as tightly packed as the soil, only hotter, exerting more pressure. He drags himself toward a group of people clustered around a guide. He cannot see the guide's face just the jut of the chin, cannot hear actual words just sounds.

He whispers to someone at the edge of the crowd, "Is there some place to get something to drink up here?" No answer. He asks a woman who looks maternal, she shakes her head without looking at him. A moment later they all applaud and make their way toward a bus. His mouth is swollen, scorched, his ears ache. The muscles responsible for bending his legs have started to shimmy, there is nothing to lean on, nor is there a place to sit down. Physically unable to retrace his steps, he requests a ride on the bus, is refused. The bus is privately owned, is full, or is going in the wrong direction. In another version he maintains that he was already too weak to cross the terrace, he saw the bus leave, he was helpless, alone.

But when the bus was out of sight, a boy appeared, so he said. The boy was playing with a piece of string, tying knots he slipped onto his fingers like nooses, pulled tight till the skin bulged red. He released the knots and started again.

He told the boy he was dying of thirst, the boy tilted his head as if he would laugh. The boy opened his mouth, made rain with his fingers—a noose dangling from his hand.

"It's not going to rain," he answered sternly. "If that's what you're trying to convey you are wrong." Not a cloud in the sky, not a hint...

In another version the boy left on the bus, jumped on the back fender and was gone. Completely alone and dying of thirst, swatting flies, sweating, great pressure from the sky...

A density like custard, defying deflection, pressed down on his limbs, he couldn't move. In this version hot pains cramp his belly, his chest—he rarely pretends to be a saint. Because he never mentions the view, one assumes he was suffering too steadily to see it. The humid pressure attacked his temples, they throbbed with the echo of his pulse. Then the air around him began to sweat, drops of water bloomed in suspension. A static mist with internal tension—hot water squeezed into air. His skin reacted by melting and stretching, it lost its elastic, went limp. His skeleton, no longer securely enclosed, turned insubstantial, uncontrollably loose. The air by this time was so dense and colorless that nothing came through, he thought he was blind. A familiar panic was whipped into motion, flooding his body in waves.

At which point he realized it was raining. Rain water rolled down his face, it was warm. He opened his mouth to the sky. The map in his hand turned soggy and tore, he let it fall to the ground.

Then he noticed someone at the edge of the parapet, was relieved he wasn't alone. She was tying a scarf, a wet scarlet cloth, fastening it under her chin. He was whistling some fragmented tune. The confusion he felt was not complex—his intelligence is so specifically adjusted that his emotions are often unaffected by it.

"Can we get a lift back down?" he called out. She was apparently startled to see him. "I hiked up," he explained holding out his limp map, he moved closer, his voice reassuring.

Dramatically raising her arm to her brow, she said a few words he did not understand. He was naturally impatient because of the rain, all he could think of was shelter, dry clothes. She repeated the same syllables slowly, carefully, as if to a child—he broke in. "There must be some other way, that damn path..." Irritation, sparked by momentary loathing, intensified by memory—he was standing too close. Sensations he could not refuse were admitted—he took her arm—she jerked it away, her face hard with suspicion. He turned and walked off down the path.

So he said.

This is the time that is wasted, he was thinking, going down the steep path in the rain. If I meet her later, she'll deny she was there—he was certain of this, though the rest of it wavered. She would say she didn't climb hills. She would say she does not wear scarlet scarves. Yet he would remind her that as she rushed past, he had tried to offer—to warn her, to stop her. The only return was the thickening rain, she disappeared from his sight soon after. A viscous curtain hung over the landscape, all detail erased.

In alternate versions he eliminates the warning, omits the rain, deletes the boy, although he retains the woman. She was standing alone at the edge of the parapet, an object or morsel of food in her palm. Or unfolding a yellow, cellophane wrapper with maddening care and concentration...

His suit soaked through, shoes caked with mud, he came back the same way he had gone. The rain had done nothing to cool the air, which, if anything, felt dirtier and heavier.

"SHE SAYS SHE HAD WAITED FOR him to return—which he has repeatedly denied. He was sullen, soaked to the bone, she says. He was frightened by the look on her face. After fixing the bed and positioning the fan, she tried to help him dry off. He jerked the towel from her hand. 'I'm perfectly capable,' he fumed. 'I'm perfectly capable,' she mimicked. Her imitations, though crass, are striking. When he got into bed, she lay down beside him, like a guest with a stranger, without speaking, he said. His eyes were closed, his breathing light, neither asleep nor pretending. She stroked his forehead to console him. The course of least resistance is dependable, flowing like water wherever it pleases. He suddenly sat up, eyes wide, jaw tense. 'What is it?' she said. He didn't answer. The only thing happening was the natural breakdown of light into shadow at the end of the day.

"Then he said the last bit of sand was going and asked her to turn the glass over. She did not return to the bed. Standing at the window, her back to the bed, completely devoid of attention, he said, she enclosed herself in a scene without him, forcing him to be no one again. The light was thin, complacent. Both time and light were being drained off together, steadily as sand seeping into the glass. His shoes were still by the door. His papers were scattered over the table, a few had blown to the floor. She picked them up and straightened them. She says she read nothing, do you trust her? There wasn't enough light to read by. Innocently pulled from task to task—her inclination to take up the slack. 'It's the heat that makes him impatient,' she said. 'It makes us all impatient,' I replied.

"Her version continued, confined to her side, an obscure uneasiness settling around her. Hours marked by simple diversions tend to leave one unaffected. She hung up his wet clothes while he slept, she said. He insists they stayed where they fell. She opened the door and looked down the hall: silence, bags of plaster, dust. At that point he called out, 'Could you bring me a cover?' She went in and found he was shivering. 'Am I sick?' he asked in the childish voice that she often found disagreeable. 'I've always worried about falling ill in foreign countries. I've had nightmares,' he confessed. She dissolved some pills in water for him, advised him to sleep if he could.

"Soon after that she left the room, ostensibly to contact a doctor. Yet he contends that she went out to dinner, leaving him completely alone. He was ill, there was no one to call. The last thing he remembered was a nightmare approaching. He tried to stop it before it unraveled. He had already seen it, knew it by heart: there was no place to sit down. The buildings were jammed against each other, the food was too spicy, the water could kill you. To say nothing of bats, foul odors and heat—what he actually remembered was the heat."

A LOW MIST HANGS OVER THE ground like steam, lit by light streaming from the cafe. Some people leave, others enter. Conversations surge and contract. Sentiments wound up like toys are set down to perform in mid-air among the tables. Conditions too slight for complete performance bear down with invisible pressure. Each breath brings minor mutations. We drink and talk about patience and illness—to ward off silence, to prove we agree. The tone of our voices, that sane verbal tide, reassures us that we agree. What pains we keep to prove it. Each cup and saucer, each glass, each postcard—no wobbly legs, no matchbooks stuck under.

Without a glance in our direction, a woman slips into a place at the bar. The air is so close you could faint. I recognize her immediately. While continuing to contribute my quota of verbiage, I watch her without seeming to notice her. Matches, dogs, ice for one's drink—pay no attention to what I am saying—one person drinks while another is talking. Nothing in her seems alert. She looks around as if we're familiar: no curiosity at all. The room, the people, the heat are transparent, inaudible, inconsequential to her. .

"Is it you?" A piercing voice—recognition. The two women eagerly embrace.

"Reunited after a decade," someone says.

The encounter changes her instantly. Animation so thoroughly transforms her appearance, I am no longer sure that I know her.

"Even artificial acts are revealing," someone says in a marginal voice.

"It *is* you!" Exclamations take time to subside. You hear the chime of eager agreement competing in a pitch of excitement. A pitch that stays bright as they hasten to outline the peculiar coincidence that brought them both here. In their rush to establish the larger picture, descriptive passages are omitted. Proper names are shed quickly in passing. The braid of their voices, their familiar inflections—her first husband, her second and so on—laughter. They buy each other drinks. "I come in for cigarettes and run into you!" she says for the third or fourth time. More laughter. I watch with perverse fascination. They light each other's cigarettes and laugh, an intimacy, a conspiracy of mutual applause. They remember friends in common events and divulge the endings of several stories that had lain dormant for years. This is combined with a list of achievements: a house, inevitable children, vacations. She leans forward and whispers her next remark—laughter springs up between them. It infects them with a curious strength. She glances at me, whispers again—their laughter turns shrill and cloying.

"If striking a match is a dress rehearsal, time and again for the great final fire..."

More laughter—I don't understand. Is she actually

looking at me—shall I wink? I'm sure I don't know her, she is not who I thought. No doubt I remind her of someone also, but I'm not in the mood for her passes. The pressure of confinement, the skill of preventing—I can turn my back on the rest and walk out.

In the doorway I pause to look back—our eyes meet. In that moment I am sure I don't know her. Then suddenly the wine glass breaks in her hand, the severed bulb bounces and breaks.

"Did she do that on purpose?"

"What's wrong with that woman?"

Holding the stem, recklessly laughing—but at least she is no longer looking at me. She picks up slivers of glass with bare fingers and drops them onto the plate of biscuits. I don't stay to see the next act.

The street is still wet, dull twilight repeated, dankness extending in every direction. I hear my own voice, its despised independence. It knows from experience I am powerless to stop it. It replays the thrill of the moment I saw her, considerably simplified already. She is not anyone I know. Yet because of her an audible disturbance is making a place for itself in my mind. Why was she looking at me? I lay this question over others, a blanket with a very tight weave.

N ANOTHER SITUATION, PRI-
vately extended, a plot in some other mind is being
settled. He follows the women along the dark road until
they go into a house. He waits. A light goes on, he pulls
himself up. With only a bamboo shade to conceal him, he
crouches on the ledge by the open window. The room is
clean as a stage set. An old velvet couch is off to one side,
a folding screen, a small ornate rug, as well as the re-
quisite table with chairs. The space among these is
excessive, isolating. Each piece is a separate island, in-
tact. When she drapes her shawl over the back of a chair,
the other dutifully picks it up and takes it out of the
room.

Now she is alone. He is tempted to put his voice into
the room—the imagined impact makes his heart pound.
Unable to hear beyond the pounding, he craves some
quick, piercing sound. The arc of a scream would be
brilliant. The walls are bare plaster, the floor is tile—
nothing but the old velvet couch to absorb it, and the
little ornate rug. He imagines his body entering that
room—a leopard springing down from a tree...

Would he want his face if he saw it now, this mask stretched over his subliminal skull, a grin as unsteady as water. The night behind him has vanished. He is nowhere if not with her in this room as she leafs through some papers on the table. Abruptly she stiffens, her eyes sweep the room. She roughly folds some papers in half, tucks them into the back of her dress. Then opening a book as if she has been reading—just as the other returns with a tray.

"Where did you pick this up?" she asks, waving the book in the air, laughing. *"Generally wayward and capricious as children, native servants must not be allowed..."*

"Pay no attention—what will you have?"

"For an extra fee you can usually arrange for the milkman to bring the cows up to the house and milk them in front of your door. In this way you will be certain that you..."

"A mere curiosity, words..."

"If your valoun is not properly aired..."

"Take this will you?" she hands her a glass. The book is returned to the table.

The substance of their conversation is radically different from what he expected. This is not what he wanted at all. Obligatory reports of external conditions are passed back and forth, devoid of passion. Their sentences are equal to each other's. From his place on the ledge, he finds himself facing the same desperation sentence after sentence, yet he stays where he is without moving. The courteous rustle of their conversation postpones the familiar wait of night, dead night as if on a dead land. He does not care what subjects they choose as long as they continue talking, holding the night at bay. The wedding car is mentioned in passing, the explosion, that trap someone found, and the chemist. This leads them to mention the clinic which...

Without warning the scene disappears. Nothing at all is seen, he is blind.

"Never mind I have candles," he hears her say and a glow appears on the table. The room is completely transformed. The table is a small planet of light in a void of a blackest night. The flame wavers without going out. He can no longer tell the women apart, the tone has turned intimate, he can barely hear them. One of them toys with candle wax, while the other is speaking so methodically that she may be reading from a book.

"See here, I've made a dog, woof woof," She laughs, drops the wax on the saucer.

"I dreamed about dogs last night, I was..."

"Listening to dreams is intolerable," she laughs.

"It was daylight. I was crossing the access when dogs—there were seven or eight coming toward me, barking and crying in unison, like chanting, singing in an open choir. I wanted to stop and listen, but as usual I was late to the clinic. They were tall and sleek, some walked on all fours, others pranced on hind legs. They were playing and singing and chanting together, one tried to lick my hand. Another offered a glass of wine..."

"Dreams. Do you know what dreams are? Life covered over with common black cloth so thin it seems transparent."

"Then one of the dogs..."

He abruptly turns away. No trace of responsibility—he is leaving. He is autonomous, he may leave. The night around him is open, not closed, he jumps down from the ledge and is gone.

CONTINUING TALK ABOUT rabbits and traps, patients at the clinic—take what you want. The cafe is crowded, stratified noise, conversations surge forward and retreat.

"False charm will eventually surface as hostility..."

"I warned her not to go there at night."

"Give him a little something to eat, he'll be licking your hand for the rest of his life."

"Don't bother, stay where you are, I'm going."

A man comes in, goes out, returns. Pursuing something with obvious reluctance—circuitous doubt, mistrust. He is large, middle-aged, and ill. The natural sensuousness of his mouth is held in check by a cigarette. Approaching a young man he speaks, the youth shrugs. The lack of social formality between them leads one to conclude they don't know one another—or else they know all too well. He gestures to the door, the youth shakes his head no.

"I knew your father quite well," someone says off to the side.

The youth follows the man to a table by a window.

The man wipes both chairs with his handkerchief quickly, the youth rolls his eyes, they sit down. Through the window come whiffs of burning rubber that blend with the smoke and the sticky saturation of used-up overbreathed air. Overhead fans try to give it a lift, it is too heavy to move.

The youth gazes out the window. The man sets forth an inaudible question, a goad from the back of his pond. No reply. The youth still gazes out the window. Other voices push their way through.

"Some sprinkle cool water on their wrists for relief—others say something nasty about others."

"Do what you like, it's not up to me, but if I were you..." The voice drops abruptly, is immediately replaced by another.

"That boy is useful to no one but himself. She should have taken his shovel and sold it, buried it under the veranda, *I* would have."

"When I arrived I made an effort..."

"No one says such things without hindsight!"

"Last week when she was buying water..."

"Last night when she came in he was reading, calm as could be, but she knew he'd been smoking..."

The dominant chord is domestic, sheltered, feeding them as they are fed in their dreams. In dreams where the grist is strung out, the ends meet—or are twisted like string around a finger, or drawn through a fist and retrieved as a scarf, that same scarf he said she tied in the rain.

The youth still gazes out the window.

The man, becoming aggressive, speaks louder. "Here's an example of what I am saying," he points to his glass on the table. "This line is made by the level of the liquid—if I take a drink, the line changes. Add water and it changes in the other direction—yet a line always remains. Anything above or below it is dismissed, is too weak to hold our attention. I'm not talking about volume—are you listening?" An indefinite violence crosses his face, the youth reluctantly turns from the window, replies with exaggerated slowness.

"And if the glass should fall off the table?"

"That's not the point, that's not what I'm saying."

"Someone standing too close to a fire comes away with scorched trousers," he replies.

"I give up. I can't—we can't talk to each other." He drains his glass, pushes it away.

Outside, a man passes by with a dog, fur plastered against its long ribs. This may be the same man—average height with hair—whose picture was in the paper. He was drawing with a stick on the ground. He was the one who unearthed a jacket, perhaps it was trousers, from the mud. He pulled a roll of bills from the pocket—as if he knew they were there, someone said. He peeled them apart, they were wet, stuck together. He kissed each one as he smoothed out the corners and spread them out on a bench. Then he lay down to sleep. It was twilight, the sky was still light at the bottom, the slats of the bench were outlined clearly against the white of his shirt. Later when they came and woke him, they made him stand up—the bills stuck to his back. Red spots all over the back of his shirt—money that bled to death on him. Directly behind him was the front-page explosion so dark it leached through the rest of his story.

"You seem to forget how well I knew him, I'm not

saying he lacked desire," says a woman. "But if no one inspired it directly, he had no extraneous passion. Thus he never needed to possess anyone, not the flesh, nor the psychic alliance around it. When he was a student..."

The youth with his head against the wall, eyes half-closed, nearly falling asleep. The older man shifting in his chair. Specific attention to indirect longing—partial disclosure, no reward for attention—he speaks sternly to the youth. "Sleep is primarily a mental activity and not a physical necessity. Sleep as a force that has its own laws, its own orbit, its own set traps for your dogs..."

The youth rubs his cheek against the rough wall, refusing to be a subject. He makes himself lost in himself. His soft flesh nestles the wall like a pillow, he appears to be asleep.

The man is increasingly restless. His left hand grazes his sickly neck, a screen for some other action or doubt. He signals the waiter, takes out some money—the currency that has molded his life, the life piling up at his feet. He no longer sifts through it daily or weekly, but leaves it to forge its own fate. Old needs spilling over each night in the wake of his temperature rising, night sweating, blue rooms...

He forces his way through the crowd to the door. From the rigid force of his ailing body one presumes he has not come to terms with the evening.

The youth immediately wakes up.

SALT FISH ON ONE PLATE, CRACK-
ers on another—submissive light, available props. No
entrance is immediately obvious. Near one's elbow is a
list of festivities, dates crossed out in pencil. On the wall
one bucket of sand is missing, its ghost, a light-scar,
inhabits the absence. The salt fish disappear one by one.

Finally he looks up. The present begins to thicken
again, breaks through his stupor, blends with his chew-
ing. Peripheral interference increases dramatically,
though he still lacks affirmation.

His companion, a woman in a dark dress, continues
speaking as if he is listening. Her words sink before they
arrive. Protecting himself, his disposition—he says he
prefers to eat without talking.

"I too prefer that," she says with more volume, the
corners of her mouth dipping downward. Is she amused?
Disappointed? Uncertainty makes him uneasy. A scrap
of silence torn from the salt fish, folded, tucked under his
tongue—if he could. He would like for once to create a
silence, to keep it, and trust it could not be undone.
Drawing the plate of crackers toward him, he arranges

them idly, sides touching, overlapping, fanning them out in a circle.

"You arrange yourself like that you know, a circle with no way to enter," she offers.

Unable to hear what she says, he shrugs, continues playing with the crackers. Why not have conspicuous agreement at least among crackers on a plate? He consciously rejects such strict forms. Yet quietly devoting himself to his circle, he begins to hear what she is saying, without noticing that he is hearing it.

"In my opinion, *she* borrowed those trousers they later found buried not far from that trap. You'd think her name was sewn into the lining, the way she didn't attempt to deny it. Then I saw in the paper that she changed her story, said she had been at the clinic that morning—that very morning she'd been thinking of leaving—which doesn't add up, you can't take things back. *She* claims she thought *all* the festivities were cancelled—shall I order more fish, are you still hungry?"

"Hunger is decorative, essential for children, invalid for us," he states.

"The way you say children suggests an aversion, stressing maturity at your age, you—a current suppressed until it explodes—you expect some flash of knowledge will do it, some arrangement of power only you comprehend—a single answer, activated hope, to fill a recently vacated position..."

Without noticing he is stopping, he stops listening. Disorganized pressures from both sides of his life expand and contract in casual cycles decreasing his ability to hear what is said. Competing authorities from both past and future squeeze him into a false parallel present—he emits empty sounds, useless gestures prevail. Words he has not had time to consider, entrenched by custom, rise up to confront him—he evades, ducks under, drifts into his own—lets her reach a conclusion without him. He offers a stuttering laugh, without mirth. She turns to admire everyone else.

The moment she glances away he stops, relieved to find himself alone.

The silence expands, he does nothing to stop it, yet he needs a impression of her at this point—an impression of laughter, of anger, no—laughter. Surely she wants to be made to laugh, for he likes the look of her laughing.

Nothing laughable appears. It is mid-afternoon and the view out the window is bleached and empty except for a dog, motionless in the gray heat. He believes he sees the dog's eyes very clearly and believes the dog sees his. Aggressively meeting the dog's steady gaze—with pristine concentration, as if not by chance, everything else is abruptly surrendered: eye-to-eye combat ensues. As a child he had often played out this challenge with both animate and inanimate partners. He knows the rules in their purity. The one who out-stares the other wins, it is a test of will and endurance. This time, however, some ballast is present, something other than will is at stake—his sanity, sexuality, his immediate autonomy. His stare turns cold with determination as he thrusts himself into the challenge. Exertion goaded by disdain for this creature, this derelict beggar with no fixed retreat—he intends to win, he believes he can force it—though some dogs have infinite patience. This dog's expression is constant, aloof, despite the mean force of the shield it encounters. The dog gives nothing for or against it—yet casually working a hole in that shield—which finally shatters as if it were glass.

He feels the dog enter his eyes, his body—a sensation calm and sacred as milk. Affection wells up in the place of disdain for this dog this presence this divinity... Give him food from the table, a place in the bed—but just at the moment he would put out his hand, the dog abruptly looks at the ground. It sniffs something there, walks away.

Disappears without looking back.

She is saying something to someone else, unaware that anything has happened without her—that he has been defeated. He needs to touch, to counter his failure, but the table has been cleared in his absence. No glasses, no crackers, no paper, no string. Distractions usually so readily available are now out of reach, the world is transparent. Surrounding him are blind statues without voices, humming so thin it is air.

Gradually some density returns. Sounds emanating from the statues thicken, glasses are raised and emptied, replaced. He crosses his legs, asserts his shoulders, his center of gravity finally shifts and a semblance of necessary conviction returns. He begins to believe he is free, autonomous, he can do whatever he chooses. He locates the cigarettes in his pocket, a convenient and acceptable procrastination. He has perfected a masculine way of cupping his hand around the flame, leaning toward it, brows tightened, swift intake—he is not oblivious to the artificial maintenance crucial to moments between larger acts.

"Are you finished?" she asks.

"Finished what?"

"That pose."

He hastily moves to restructure himself—*she is easily dismissed*—he swallows. *Under normal circumstances I would walk out*—consolation without conviction.

"Your social management, conspicuous attitudes—you must see it's useless by now. Other occasions you've previously squandered..." She lets him know he has squandered quite a few, they seethe in a heap at his feet.

He agrees—inaudible reluctance. Yet one agreement encourages another, as if agreement is all she is seeking, as if agreement is her destination. She pulls him along through a series of agreements, her voice secreting an ease which he follows. Small comfortable opinions presented in passing—a plan evolves as if it were fate. He agrees with whatever she says.

By the time they stand up and leave together, it appears that they always leave together—that it is always late afternoon.

I T IS NOT AFTERNOON BUT NIGHT.
Streetlights define the location. Nothing moves. The
kiosks along the access are closed, the canvas flaps have
been unfurled and tucked under the skeletal bodies. The
heat even at this hour and the stench—you cannot
discount either one. Heat, which makes one need to
move slowly, the stench, which makes one need to move
fast...

Rotating from one's feet are quick shadows that lead,
are walked over and obliged to follow before coming back
to the lead. He notices now with a quick lift of pride how
his shadow is broad and well-defined, while hers is nearly
transparent.

"You live on one of the better streets," he hears
himself observe.

"Imagine whatever you like."

A wave of tension provoked by her voice ripples
through him before it subsides. This tremor is followed
by another that is stronger, affecting the area of his solar
plexus. *Imagine whatever you like! Imagine!* An excess
of energy accumulates within him, spiraling upward,

seeking escape. He tightens his chest against it. Incipient convulsions finger his muscles, he stiffens his belly to thwart them. He knows the madness of this kind of laugh, its unwieldy strength, he has suffered it before. Once it finds a way into the world, he cannot control it, that laugh takes him over.

He swallows, forcing it down. Keeps swallowing. Muscle by muscle he dismantles the tension, flattening the laugh, limiting the disruption. At the end the remaining fragments coalesce, are released in a long even sigh.

Compliant, he follows her up. She unlocks the door without shifting her tone. "In your attempt to deny limitations you make the assumptions that everyone makes. Reproducing motion through memory or habit, you move the same story through the same verbs and the same predetermined restrictions apply. Pleasure alternates with despair—each bitter most-craving and irregular beauty—not beauty for the sake of beauty understand, but a force that encourages one to keep going..."

He pays no attention at all. Glancing at the room as he enters, he is no longer certain she lives alone. He tries to see through the wall of time for a glimpse of who had been here before him. Flies graze on crumbs on the table. There are too many chairs, some, apparently broken, lean against the far wall. Through an open door at the end he sees light, strains of Western band music are audible— she immediately closes that door. Again he becomes uncomfortable in her presence, at odds with vague motives, no entrance, no approval. He picks up a book reads aloud. *"The water from any wells on the premises ought to be analyzed before being used. Water ought to be drawn off for a week, the well itself properly..."* He turns several pages at once. *"One's past sensibilities ought not be allowed to openly conflict with one's current values. Harmony depends on balance. If you cannot engage a decorator and must rely on your personal taste..."*

"Do you find that interesting?" she interrupts, reaching for a bottle under the sink, which she opens, takes a long drink. He sees she is independent of him, she is natural, as if he is not in the room—while he has become unbearably aware of the space of his body, its mass on the chair. As he realizes how little she depends on him, an apathy begins and expands in him, turning him into an object. She is the subject as she drinks from the bottle and his eyes cannot stray from the sight of her. Cannot blink, cannot speak without her permission—he is frozen in place as sentenced. But when she wipes off the mouth of the bottle and hands it to him, he obediently takes it.

"Too bitter?" she suggests.

"Perhaps." The sound of his voice reassures him. He finds he can change the position of his chair, become more compatible, invite her favor. An overhead fan stirs the air without ceasing, but still he is hot, he takes off his shirt, throws it on the floor behind him. She moves to a stool by the window. He cannot see her face without turning.

"I suppose you want to know more about me, my relations with—others—my part in the story," he says in a cautious voice.

"The distance between inventing and recalling isn't a vacuum you know," she replies.

"I didn't say it was," he defends. "As a child I was haunted by certain accusations..." Eager to open his sacred material, he issues a rush of dry air with his words.

One small opening is all he maintains, the same hole every time he goes in. Approaching familiar ancestral markers, he divulges the sins of familial culprits—coldness, stupidity, untimely distress—he pauses for it to sink in. But as if the suffering of childhood were voluntary, she offers no sympathy, no consolation. He turns around in his chair. "Aren't you listening?"

"Familiar articles don't need inspection each time you happen to see them again. Your requirements are extraordinary." She looks at him squarely, he looks back—their eyes lock. He struggles to stay—she holds firm.

A simple yawn cracks his resolve.

While she is washing her hands at the sink, he notices the postcard tucked in the mirror, is reminded of something, some phrase she wrote. He can see the pen in her hand, its shadow, the postcard beneath her left fist. The table is round, not wood, but gray marble—he pumps the image for more. He pushes his fingers into his eyes, making sparks that contribute nothing. He tries to reclaim the original picture—finds the way blocked by a word. The word table has taken the place of that table and he cannot see anything, not wood, not marble, nor can he see her hand. He has only an audible expanse without substance, a string of sound from postcard to hand.

Then abruptly abandoning that mental alcove, he surges ahead to some possible future. He sees twilight out the window, his own window. He is waiting for her to come home. She comes home. He tilts his head for her kiss, takes her hands—she smiles because she is pleased to see him. How simply it happens in the future. These decoys only partially suspected—little places with act-ing, a thirst set apart—but they vanish the moment she speaks.

"What do you want?" she asks.

The empty space that waits for an answer is definite and pulls him back into the present. And although he sincerely would like reply, he finds the center of her question blind. What does *she* want him to want? Inaudibly he questions the question. Two inquiries, traveling on parallel ropes, move in opposite directions. He craves a place to sit down in the center—suspended, composed, in the center of both. But he is addicted to immediate success and flattering images of himself. He absently picks up a scrap of paper and winds it on his finger. The subject becomes his finger. So many subjects of interest on a body—the peculiar way a nail has grown in, the hard knot at the base of a neck. So many fine flaws that are part of a history—proof of participation in life. "I remember when I got this scar," he says cutting into the silence.

In front of him numerous flies are struggling to throw off the stupor induced by the liquid she casually sprayed on the table. Many flies are already calm. She sweeps them all off the table together, a task performed with oblique displeasure, gestures trance-like, aggressive indifference. He finds himself powerless again. Finds it impossible to avert his gaze as she sweeps the flies into a bucket of sand. With a flick of her wrist they are buried. She hangs the bucket on the wall. She does not look in his direction, does not acknowledge his presence—which provokes him. What is he doing in this room at this table? Why did he come here with her? As the recipient of her displeasure, he feels responsible for it. Yet how steadily she pushes him back! The motion with which she is scrubbing the table grinds her dissatisfaction deeper. He sees it at the corners of her mouth. At the back of his mind he hears her ask, *Shall we go somewhere else?* He imagines her shrewdly leading him back to the cafe, they go in for a drink, she excuses herself, disappears down the hall—there's a passage to the alley through the cellar. This ancient remedy so easily recited at predictable intervals remains effective. He clears his throat rudely, she finally looks up—he notices the hat in her hand. *Shall we go?* She is trying the hat backward and forward in the mirror, varying the tilt, he cannot see her face.

"I'm not responsible for your flies," he says flatly.

"Why can't you be more objective?" Her eyes are on herself in the mirror, she fans her hair out at the sides. "If certain genders were reversed..."

Habitually accustomed to hearing the worst, he concludes he is wrong, thus inconsequential. He occupies the center of nothing. His location in the world is arbitrary, his life, though luminous for himself, is expendable, a mere backdrop for everyone else. His head drops onto his arms on the table. His watch ticks in his ear.

The medicinal odor of soap brings him back. Again she is washing her hands at the sink. "These drains have always given us trouble from the day we moved in—is it like this all over?"

The new configuration jolts him. Who is the other half of *we*? He feels the question so acutely that he cannot bring himself to utter it. He had relied on her being as he is, deliberately separate from everyone else. Yet, even as he recoils from this jolt, he knows that he knew all along. The other half of her equation has been taunting him all evening. "Why don't you ask me to leave?" he says bluntly.

"Is that what you want?"

"I have my own affairs to look after." He picks up his shirt from the floor.

"Some people are isolated by what they possess, others by what they haven't received. I've offered you food and a place for the night..."

And that other person you keep by your side, have you offered me him or her as well? he asks silently buttoning his shirt. *Something to eat and a place to sleep out of pity,* he thinks, impatient to leave. The prospect of intimacy has vanished. Because she is balanced by somebody else, both her background and foreground exist in one place. He utters a perfunctory "good night" at the door.

"That is one version, there are others," she reminds him.

He does not ask what they are.

NOTHING REMAINS BUT TO finish packing and buy something to eat on the train. Saltines, a few tins of fish, lemonade. Abandoning the papers spread out on the table, he heads for the market by way of the access, ignoring the more direct route. Either he is unfamiliar with it, or he has forgotten the time.

Low, passive structures all around. The road meanders without reward among bleached walls, solid gates, no shade. An unseen dog snarls, then another. Above, isolated from everyone else, a figure on a balcony sinks to the tiles. Farther along a woman is calling out, "Joseph!" to a youth who is walking away. Framed by a window behind a black grille, she appears to be wearing a native costume, hair tucked under a bright bandanna, a colorful blouse—but he didn't bring his camera. She continues calling: "Joseph! Joseph!" The boy is already out of the picture.

As he resumes his trek to the market, her shrill voice turns melancholic. He strolls as if for the sake of hearing it gradually fade in the distance.

A glance at his watch wakes him up. How did it get

so late? His train leaves in less than two hours. He has misplaced a segment of time, or his watch—he shakes his wrist and listens. The market is still quite far. "Why didn't you take a car?" he mutters. "Now that you have to rush. Grab something, anything at all, at the market—pack and shower, pack, pay the bill, pack and get to the station, no, I won't have time to shower."

Yet bathing has been on his mind since waking, drumming water easing his shoulders—and the air after bathing is fresher, sweeter—he mentally retrieves the jar of water he keeps wrapped in wet towels on the floor. He lies down on the bed by the window to drink it—is abruptly returned to the heat of the street and the struggle to keep walking faster. "I never have enough time," he mutters, complaint, not regret, in his tone.

When I arrived I made an effort...

Some effort those postcards you sent, that message: Climate abominable, inhabitants insufferable—wish you were here.

It's actually not bad, not that unattractive, I don't hate it, I just can't—feel comfortable here...

As if you feel comfortable everywhere else.

It's the heat, it's impossible to explain how the heat...

Habitual exchanges pried open, snapped shut. His breathing turns short, he is sweating profusely—no shade at all at this hour. The road is much longer than it seemed at the start, it is taking too long to get there. *Walk faster, damn you, can't you walk any faster?* Forcing his legs to move more quickly—the ground beneath him turns into a treadmill.

I could pass out right here in the road...

You aren't going to pass out, you're fine, it's nothing.

He imagines falling to the ground. Some boys approach, not ones he knows, a hand slips into his billfold pocket...

"It's not going to happen," he objects.

They find you half-dead in the middle of the street, haul you off to the clinic...

"It's not!"

Hose you down with disinfectant, inject what they inject in others...

He jerks his head but the image floats back: bare walls, the razor top fence, locked doors. As if that vision of his future is permanently glued to the back of the present moment, no space between, a premonition—he quickens his step.

You won't pass out, you're fine.

I won't pass out, I'm just tired. Slight indigestion, the milk, the oysters...

The milk was sour, you've had it before.

Of course I will, I don't miss trains.

You've always managed...

Of course I have managed!

Locking himself into a hopeful present, he enters the market as if he is calm, plows through the dank alley, caged animals, caged birds, blue smoke from a spit, he is fine. Nothing disturbs his forced mood. It is not until he is waiting in line that impatience fingers his nerves again. "Damn it you're taking all day!" he cries out. The woman continues counting aloud, the bills stick together, she has to start over. He still needs to buy crackers, he won't trust their bread, these flies, their hands, he's afraid to get sick. He wants a tin of factory-sealed crackers, officially stamped, internationally approved.

As he approaches the covered storehouse, he notices the woman standing outside. With extremely slow deliberate gestures she is unwrapping something he cannot make out. He knows he has seen her before, but can't place her, nor does he take time to try. He rushes inside and buys the saltines, finds a driver who takes him back to the hotel—all the while avoiding his watch. He will not admit that rushing is futile, time has run out, the train is leaving. He thrusts himself forward, intentions knotted, his lower back cast in cement. He has had other experiences like this, but someone else had always been there to draw back the curtain, interpret the view, fold his shirts neatly and pack them.

He stuffs his clothes in the bag, his papers—he still has to settle his bill...

When the driver tells him the train has departed, he defiantly refuses to believe it. He insists that the driver take him to the station and he settles in back with his luggage beside him. The driver reluctantly starts out.

Because of the festival, the road is crowded and the driver will not use his horn. No breeze through the window, surrounded by bodies—the car moves grudgingly ahead. As if the train is mystically connected to the hands on his watch, he avoids his watch. He sets his sight on a vision of the station, the train at the platform—he strains to hold it. In his effort to make the scene more authentic, he adds details: white billowing steam, old porters. A woman wearing a colorful scarf is weeping and waveing to a man who is leaving. The difficulty of maintaining this vision is compounded by the drone of the driver's voice. A man is walking alongside the car and the driver is conversing with him.

"He won't believe the train has left, got in back, and wouldn't budge. I charge double for futile excursions, I told him."

"Triple for missing a train." They laugh.

He can see the back of the driver's head supported by a gray chunk of neck. Dark glasses in the rear mirror. The driver's voice occurs unattached, somewhere near the mirror. The other voice drifts through the window—a pillow-like torso with a common leather strap is all that is available. The passenger has been made insignificant, driver and pedestrian proceed without him. He realizes that traveling is always like this—sitting in back without any water. *This is the reason you don't like to travel, this is why people stay home.* He remembers the jar under the sink wrapped in towels—he hadn't had time to drink it.

The platform is empty and the station deserted, it is obvious that the train has departed. A few sturdy boys with bulging pockets stand at the corner—the driver turns. "I suppose you want to go back," he says smugly over his shoulder.

"What time does the train leave tomorrow?"

"It's a holiday."

"The day after?"

"That too."

Finally he has to let go of his plan, release his intentions—give in. The plan lingers in a thin, methodical state before disappearing entirely.

Nothing appears in its place.

The car lumbers back through throngs of people—no plan, no diversion, a blank tomorrow. Time is slack all around.

Without looking at the driver, without further words, he pays what is asked, carries in his own luggage. The same room, the same sheets, the same towels on the floor—but the jar of water is missing.

Nothing to do but lie down and sleep, he is useless at this point, as if buried. Right away a vision or a dream invades him—he is beginning to know it by heart. The hill is steep, he climbs steadily. The air is a sweltering mass of yellow—his throat is parched, he cannot find shade. Hot pains cramp his belly, he has trouble breathing—at which point he sees he is not alone. A woman he has seen before is waiting for him off to one side. He moves toward her, calling out, "I am ill." She looks at him with ambiguous compassion. *Customs may be easy to follow but appetites are difficult to conceal.* She offers him something in a cellophane wrapper—which he accepts. She vanishes. In another version, a boy appears, it rains, he gets soaked, he loses his map as he makes his way back down the path. Coming out on the road on the far side of the access—a wedding car passes, it is dusk. He goes back along that same road again, in limited light, dogs bark, nothing moves...

The ends of the dream pass back and forth so lightly that nothing is felt, nothing remains. Soft ground accepts both shovels and spoons, whatever is handy for digging the pit that he throws the towel into after. Entire structures are dismantled each night, only to rise again in the morning. Night in most countries is closed. Sleep, by necessity, is closed. The day pulled out from under his feet catches fire, burns out of control as he sleeps. The wedding car jerks to a halt once again, is set on fire, turned into a hearse—but he sleeps.

"THE MOST STRIKING FEATURE was the care—the attention—visible in its construction. Though she called it a trap, it was obviously too fragile, wound string held the corners together. The bars were evenly honed. Bars with the muscle of twigs—some trap. She had to admit it was more like a cage. The rain had just stopped, she was drenched. She said she had tried to flag down a bus, the wedding car passed, it was dusk..."

He is leaning against a tree as he speaks, barely separate from the dark background. The sun has long passed the horizon. A dog approaches—he lurches to kick it. It jumps back with a yelp, slinks away. "You don't need to use my version, there are others. In one, she was dressed as a man. In another, I was confused with the chemist. We're apparently about the same size, the same age, with similar addictions," he laughs.

We grapple with the implication.

His speech adjusts to accommodate our doubt. "You are welcome to question the accuracy of my memory, but the fact is—and let me define the word *fact*..."

His voice is replaced by another, closer: "Is there

some place to get something to drink?" He asks again. I shake my head no. He asks for a match. I shove some matches into his palm. But the matches initiate a peripheral ritual, he searches his pockets for cigarettes and so on. At the end he insists on returning the matches—only to ask to use them again. What's wrong with him, is he doing this on purpose? I miss the rest of what was being said.

"It's common to want to return to a site where something traumatic has occurred," someone says.

"The point that I was making," he says.

"An attempt to retouch old sentiments that..."

"I wasn't supposing I was merely suggesting..."

"Is there some place to get something to drink around here?" the fellow asks in a louder voice, addressing the entire company. Dogs, matches, something to drink—sand that seeps through the fingers.

"Come to my room, I have plenty to drink," the man by the tree announces broadly, his manner unexpectedly expansive.

Without much discussion, we decide to go with him, though a few discreetly withdraw. As we walk he mentions the red scarf she was wearing, how it bled when she wrung it—I don't hear the rest. By my side is the fellow who asked for the match, now he asks my name, address, occupation—how long have I been here and so on. He insists his curiosity is idle, impersonal—his vehemence makes me suspicious. I push ahead to catch up with the others.

"How did you manage to get the best room?" someone asks as we enter, the walls are bright blue.

"Is it the best?" he asks.

The light is excessive, even painful. Texture is obliterated by it, all roughness, all smoothness erased. A hard outline backs up each object—his chairs, his cases, his books, his clock are compressed and materialized by the light. The surrounding space of gelatinous time does nothing to keep them in place. There are no barking dogs in the distance, no distance here in this room.

Not only has our setting changed, but the mood is more artificial. Now we are individuals, separate, contradictory ambitions revive. Yet soon we begin taking sides, the same side. This is, after all, his room and not ours. The view from this window like the view from his eyes— and the stories he scatters so freely around him—all verify him and not us. We stand over here, he stands over there. When he tries to restore his position of authority, he finds us blocking the way. As if we are teasing, he elbows in—we elbow him out the same way. He obviously wants to say something conclusive, the cold-metal solace of a closed circle—I hear it in his voice.

We blatantly ignore him for several minutes. Someone lies down on his bed. He fixes a harmless concoction with syrup and aerated water for us. It is not hard to refuse. "There's always water at the hotel," he says as if this is the reason he came. "There is always electricity as well." His words sound monitored in this bleached space. His confidence has deteriorated to arrogance. Someone is joking behind his back—laughter turns finicky and spurious. We talk among ourselves about things that happened before he arrived. Naturally the chemist's wife is mentioned.

"How well did you know the chemist?" he probes, false innocence padding the tone.

"Know him—I've kissed him!" she answers. We laugh in an unfriendly way.

"A kiss is a truce, a trap, or a link—a deposit whose worth is offset by intention..."

"Consider your own intention," someone tells him.

"I hear you went to the clinic last week," I say bluntly, avoiding his eyes. The others stop talking to listen.

"A simple intestinal weakness, it was nothing."

"Intentional weakness."

"Conventional sweetness."

"A normal reaction, you can look at the flies," he says and we joke about files and flies. This seems to change things, this joking together.

"In my opinion..." he starts up again. Someone immediately interrupts.

"Opinions are sentiments made of rubber—they expand to fit over any protrusion."

"If air is too hot you turn on a fan, if water is too cold you heat it." Someone laughs, but the line is dropped.

"Is there more ice?"

"Let me finish!" he complains. "There's more to what I have said than you give..."

"What is more is a truce, a trap, a link, a deposit whose worth is defiled by intention."

"The day I was caught in the rain..." he breaks through. But he pauses and in that pause we go in, grinding our words against his, gaining ground. The ground, always subject to change, begins changing, his subject is ground to a halt.

THE LITTLE LAMP LIT IN THE corner for justice allows enough light to come through. Ancient light and tall wavering shadows, shadows touched with the left hand. Along with the books within easy reach are curious articles spread out on the table. She keeps them, she has said, for tomorrow. She speaks of tomorrow as a definite location, as if she could go to its door any time, turn the knob and walk into tomorrow. "Tomorrow we shall go to the station," she states with inflexible confidence. "The drains shall be fixed tomorrow."

Yet despite her sureness, the air in the passage that leads to tomorrow occasionally thickens. She has to push to get through it. A concentration accumulates around her as the present thickens and blocks out tomorrow. Severe fluctuations of intention occur, she makes frequent trips to the cupboard. Each time she attempts to identify this affliction, she offers a word, which she sets in its place: apathy, dread, irritation and so on. The word, an antidote for the condition, moderates the pressure and the isolation, and elicits hope in her favor.

It is dread she says, it is only dread. And she goes on with what she was doing.

Because she does not trust the servants she keeps the keys to the clock in her pocket. She winds and rewinds that clock. She reads from the book on the table. *Your meat-safe must have plenty of air without being exposed to sun. The sides must be perforated zinc. The legs must stand in tins of water and the back should not touch the wall. Your servants must clean the shelves daily. Their habit of cramming lamp rags and candle ends into the drawers must be prevented...*

If someone has entered the room behind her she has not heard and continues reading. For the moment her affliction is wrapped, a soft parcel, a lapsed contract on a back shelf. *Most ladies will provide gloves for their servants, which she has purchased herself. Native servants, if left to buy their own gloves...*

She hears him behind her, continues reading.

...the finger tips, beyond his control, will find their way into each plate of soup.

"Some natives will be discreetly rewarded—may blossoms fall on their heads," he says, dropping into a chair beside her. "Does anyone do anything humble by choice—down planks without steps, honest work anymore?" He reads aloud over her shoulder. "*Some natives will try to support aged parents and other relations as well as his wife's and numerous illegitimate children. You will earnestly have to exert your authority to prevent lazy brothers from sponging on him...*"

"Is kindness essential?" he interrupts his reading.

"Can idleness be cured?" she replies.

"One hopes that history is something more than a

fashionable explanation of events. Events dried out, measured and bagged—steeped like tea and swallowed for pleasure."

She crosses the room, putting distance between them, but his voice, compact with anger, follows: "*It isn't uncommon to calm the children by administering drugs in very small doses.* It's a kindness to send them off to sleep with the sign of the cross, a kiss on the pillow."

She leaves the room without hearing the rest, he slumps in the chair, exhausted.

A few minutes later she returns with a tray, glasses, and a pitcher with ice. All of it has happened before. Time that is still and yet passively extended passes gradually through its own center. A day or another just like it is ending, voices rise and come to a halt, start up again in the next room.

They are drinking to coat their raw nerves.

Below the sensation of tepid despair, tight fists of fear grip the pulp of their spines. A host of soft shadows bent slightly at the waist, more lyrical than functional, brush against them.

PUBLIC GROUND IS NO LONGER
sacred. The access is littered with abandoned material:
paper, glass, lamp rags, shells. Fallen blossoms mistaken
for crumbs. Accumulation takes over. From this side an
entrance is barely visible. A woman stands by a corru-
gated stall, unwrapping some morsel she holds in her
hand, peeling off the tight cellophane skin.

"Damn it you're talking all day!"

Some people who hear him are thrilled. The hardened
voice, conspicuous authority—the hotel is closed, the
station gutted, puddles of glass and debris clog the roads—
yet a show of authority and conviction still thrills them.
His hands are shoved deep in his pockets.

"Relax," she says with exaggerated lightness.

He picks up the suitcase from the ground and walks
off.

"One more convention," she says catching up. "Seeing the way you walk when you're angry—I understand
why soldiers march."

His lips press rigidly together. Images from the back
of his mind are jerked into view, but denied extension,

they offer no assistance, no escape. He pretends he is walking alone. His past winds around the throat of the present so tightly he becomes parenthetical. One foot decisively in front of the other, he marches steadily toward the cafe.

By the time she arrives, he has downed his first drink. The substance, greedily absorbed by his cells, has spread through his body and into his brain. He rediscovers his flexible body. He begins to see where he is.

"What do you have there?" he asks over her shoulder. She holds up a pair of men's shoes. Glancing down he makes sure they are not his.

"Some fellow on the street—they weren't new, they were cheap. For my father—or shall I give them to you?"

He slips off his own to try them. His feet, unrestricted, pulsate with pleasure. "I'll never wear shoes again," he announces. "Not yours, not mine, not anyone's shoes." His mouth is open, tied back in a grin. This new expression displaces the previous, he is neither somber nor penitent. Protected now by a little oblivion, essential as water is to concrete, he calls out to the waiter, laughing. "Anything besides water on the menu?" People look up, then ignore him.

"No harm in a little amusement," one murmurs. Old plots like old trees—reassuring.

"I'm the one who planted those trees..."

"I've always liked a distant horizon..."

"She laughed in a way that I sensed was habitual—melodious nerves, the chemist's late wife."

"Enchantment is more important than comfort," he says, overriding the other voices. "I don't need to eat after all."

"You always say that initially."

"A world devoted to external vision will always be threatened by inner enchantment."

"There are never enough places to sit down," someone states.

"Doctors here make rounds for the scenery—did you expect to find saints? Unsupervised doses exchanged in the shadows account for what gets done in the dark. The innocence of the victims is comic, so polished—according to some of the doctors. In my opinion their watches run backwards, in my opinion there's not enough hope..."

Setting his hands on her shoulders lightly with seductive down-shifted humor he reminds her: "You said that you would tide me over with a meal and a place for the night."

"That's true."

"At what price?" he wants to know.

As a person he has the usual themes, as a man he will try to stand at her side. When she fails to answer him quickly enough, he seeks another connection. He sees a dog, stock still in the road, which reminds him of something he heard or witnessed—a memory not disagreeable, but useless. He puts back on his shoes. "I hear you got one of the better houses. Exemplary ancestors no doubt," he offers.

"I hear you have nothing at all."

"Ordinary appetites placed on an altar burned to indifferent ash."

"Indifference that disguises..."

"Indulgence has flaws."

"I come in for cigarettes and run into you!" a woman near them cries out.

"The pressure of refinement, the thrill of torment-ing..."

"...other people at other tables drink from more innocent vessels always."

The sound of breaking glass makes them turn—a woman waving a broken stem is laughing defiantly, she is helpless against it.

"Snapped it with her bare hand."

Still laughing she picks up the scattered pieces, drops them onto her plate. He watches with unconcealed fascination the careless way she retrieves the sharp shards. Without realizing that he is trapped, he is trapped—the entire scene is played out for his benefit, he is alone in the audience.

At FIRST HIS STATE OF MIND is mechanical, foot-tapping, confined to definite surroundings. For some people place is adventure enough but for him time passes too slowly. In moments like this, when place is oppressive, he craves indefinite night. He longs for lines that cannot be traced, that leave no residue, tender no loss.

Some moments slip away, others hold. A surge of hope followed by caution—another version of himself emerges.

It is her turn to offer a subject and he believes she should do so in his favor. Anticipating ice, more liquid, conclusion, he spreads himself out on the dark velvet couch. He requires a little attention at this point, though he is not ready to be grateful. Worn down by repetitious acts, by caution, fear and the tearing crosstalk, by her constant intervention, by his own inattention—some moods remain fluid, some harden.

She comes in with the tray sets it down. "Most men I've met have specialized," she informs him. She is not fatigued by obligatory measures, nor hindered by lack of attention. Her position is orderly and obvious. He hears the orderliness, not the sentence, and is driven to interrupt.

"There were two, then six, then twenty rabbits— then nineteen, eighteen, seventeen," he laughs. If confidence can be bolstered by numbers and strengthened by facts, one is able to quote, he opens the book and reads aloud in a confident voice. *"One's servant should sleep within calling distance, a light or two kept burning all night..."*

"Even pain-hardened travelers succumb to this heat," she muses. He continues.

"Your female servant is responsible for the safe custody of your personal belongings. If small articles should disappear, you must dismiss her immediately. Even if she is not the culprit, she has proved herself incapable of protecting..." He snaps the book shut, returns it to the table.

She begins talking as anyone might at the end of a day to someone familiar. Her subjects are simple, artificially prolonged, impressions of local conditions. He gazes at the ceiling as she talks. Having given her the conversation, its reach, its shape and basic direction, he makes no attempt to regain it. He drinks what he has been given to drink, one sip after another. Luxury, he thinks, is confining. He removes himself by winding his watch, a minor gesture that extends his boundary. He unbuttons his shirt, unlatches his belt. A sequence of provocative assertions follow, neither refused nor encouraged.

"You seem to me...your manner suggests...it appears that you..." A litany already exhausted. Her skillful hands caress his neck, he begins to count backward from one hundred.

But when she says, "If I were you…" he becomes alert, the equation provokes him. The *you* made equal to *I*—he stops counting. Assumptions of equality, though tempting, gall him. Based on the improbable condition that an *I* could actually be *you*—she keeps talking. Later he might recall other aspects, adjacent transactions he initially missed—he might say she intentionally made him equal just to see if he could endure it.

But unable to deny her, he is forced to contend with the possibility that she could be him. Persistently trying to enter his body, to become him, to direct and confirm from within those things that have been exclusively his—she does not stop moving closer. If she succeeds, he will become her, an opportunity he thoroughly rejects. He tries to loosen the connection she is forging—tries to rise and falls back on the cushions. She speaks with the confidence of someone accustomed to entering regions he rightfully controls, his private sector, his emotional bank. She speaks as if she has been there before—and he hears what she says and is powerless to stop her.

Simultaneously, however, she employs a disguise that makes her conversation conventional. Anyone listening would hear the convention—the strength of her smile becomes tedious. If efforts of will were mistaken for affection—yet an act of defiance would be useless at this point. What he longs for is a soft core of bliss, an amorphous substance in which to stretch out. He tries to cordon off this longing, he intends to be stable, defiant. "I frequently bathed in cold water as a child even in winter—our winters were cold," he says in the voice of a man who is drowning. He excuses himself, leaves the room.

Here, finally, is the solitude he craves. A small window opens outward to a view of the background, on the sill blossoms wilt like old snow. He looks out at a pit the size of a grave being dug by a youth in the last light of day. A voice shouts suddenly, "Get away from that window."

Stunned, he draws back out of sight.

The simplest routines are the most difficult to observe: he rinses his face at the sink. On the ledge are inevitable articles for bathing, functional, daily paraphernalia. In this setting, however, with the smell of turned earth and the barking of dogs drifting in through the window, a memory taunts him like an echo, not entirely available. He listens with his eyes. Isolating each component—the badger brush, a green packet of blades—he attempts to locate that echo, make it stronger. The razor, a blue plastic T, evokes nothing, the match book the same, dark medicinal soap... He recalls the thrill of something falling—a glass? a comb?—dull thump, not a shatter. He deliberately drops the brush on the floor, takes in the soft thud—it is close. He brings the brush close to his face to examine—abruptly returns it to the shelf.

It is natural that this memory is false, obscuring the more perfect appeal beneath it. For instance: Whose face do these articles shave? Beside the brush is a translucent cube, inexact, shallow slits in the sides. Then something moves, he turns quickly to the window—the bird flies away, disappears. Those blossoms, he sees now, are crumbs.

In an effort to keep from slipping back farther, he returns to the place where she waits on the couch.

"WHAT REMAINS IS AN URGE TO enter more fully—"

"Lemonade is more wholesome than most medication."

"Here one may have either sparrows or pleasure— one trap set without, one trap set within."

Beneath the words is a gnawing desire for something more than what has been said. Blame the heat for those flashes of irritation: "It's not *my* fault, I didn't make the climate..."

Each word, each sentence, a shift toward destruction: the inevitable pressure of confinement. Some cling to warm bodies, wake up in the dark—even passion in this climate is elastic. The human smell of human bodies, the animal smell of animal bodies—or a long slow voice entombing sentences lifted from a book on one's lap. What follows is an interval of odorless dreams moving like pages that will not stay turned.

"What will you listen to if I stop talking?" she asked when he had said nothing.

Having watched him slosh in and out of black water,

completely exposed to both light and dark—and in some other excerpt, her head on his chest, hearing his voice through his bones, she had loved him. His voice like water in canvas buckets kept in the shade was deeply refreshing. "I loved every word he said," she tells me.

"Is there more ice—even that?"

She says yes.

In the background they are devouring oysters, in the foreground an indication of music. Strong voices contaminated by sturdy subjects press into the cracks of the pauses between us. A shifting horizontal drone. Companions appear, disappear and return. Certain subjects turn luminous briefly, then fade throughout each small afternoon.

"Yet I hardly knew him," she persists. "When the fever reached its peak, he said that words broke open, spilling out their soft centers. He could taste, he could feel the soft meat of each word, he could sometimes lie down in their breath. But at the center of each center what he discovered was a pinhole through which life was steadily rushing. In that state he was powerless to stop it. He didn't dare brush the flies from his face for fear he himself would be flushed through that hole. Now he refers to that state as a spell and pretends he has a transplanted heart—a transplanted heart that lacks the experience of a pigeon tamed since birth in the breast. This confirms his condition of separation, provides an excuse to assert his difference. He quit blaming the heat, blaming the light, now that he has invented that pigeon...

"But I sensed a difference that evening," she continues. "His doubts, his obsessive sucking on air, and his jokes—subtle insults disabling his ego, scattered laughter, uncalled for explosions. He unbuttoned his shirt, the air was water, his shirt in the moonlight parted like curtains, his head was back, his face full of silver—of course I loved him, I wanted him with me! I offered myself that moment—he laughed. You could say I was some other person that evening. Then later when I came back to myself, the self that you know, the self that is speaking—you have to shout to be heard in this place!"

Jokes punctuated by rounds of applause, laughter, a background official announcement—approval followed by vague indecision, she lets this cut into the flesh of her story, which she frees with a jerk of her hand.

Long shafts of afternoon light grip the wall, a dog moves out of the shadows. "Add one more sentence, write love, sign your name," someone says with a burst of resilience. Everyone else keeps on talking. Her companion grabs the postcard and scribbles: "I know who I am, I'm aware of the room, the people here, your face, I'm not ill."

The setting resumes its familiar slow speed, the incident is all but forgotten. The clatter of dishes and smoke hems us in. Still a fragile substructure of longing is present in each glass of amber going down. I pick up the newspaper again. Here is the picture of a man at the station whose name some say is Joseph. The grain is conspicuous, you can't see his features, his suit, his case—like soot from the cellar.

I remember that cellar, there were mice. The alley behind it led to the access—bleached rubble, shattered glass, rusted buckets, sand. One image induces another. Relocating *glass* at the back of my mind, I see it exactly as I first saw it: lifted to the lips returned to the table, a little closer to the edge of the table. His fingers slide down the wet cylinder. Repetition, double voices, interpretation is impossible. The surface, as if it is liquid, trembles, deflecting what passes beyond it.